PURE
SLUSH
BOOKS

WRONG WAY

PURE SLUSH VOL. 19

GO BACK

First published as a collection October 2020
Content copyright © Pure Slush Books and individual authors
Edited by Matt Potter

BP#00097

Pure Slush Books
32 Meredith Street
Sefton Park SA 5083
Australia

Email: edpureslush@live.com.au
Website: https://pureslush.com/
Store: https://pureslush.com/store/

Original front cover design copyright © Matt Potter

ISBN: 978-1-922427-06-9

Also available as an eBook
ISBN: 978-1-922427-07-6

A note on differences in punctuation and spelling

Pure Slush Books proudly features writers from all over the English-speaking world.
Some speak and write English as their first language, while for others, it's their second
or third or even fourth language. Naturally, across all versions of English, there are
differences in punctuation and spelling, and even in meaning. These differences are
reflected in the work *Pure Slush Books* publishes, and they account for any
differences in punctuation, spelling and meaning found within these pages.

Pure Slush Books is a member of the
Bequem Publishing collective
http://www.bequempublishing.com/

• Alex Reece ABBOTT • Ahmed M. AL-ASA'ADI • Tobi ALFIER • Gemma AL-KHAYAT • Diana ALLGAIR • Sandra ARNOLD • Angelo AUCIELLO • Cathie AYLMER • Jacqueline BARTLE • James BELL • Dev BERGER • John BOST • Howard BROWN • Anika CARPENTER • Steve CARR • Anne CASEY • Chuka Susan CHESNEY • Kersten CHRISTIANSON • Jan CHRONISTER • Dave CLARK • Bethany CODY • Peter COLLINS • Lisa COLLYER • David COOK • Georgia COOK • Tony DALY • Charles N. deGRAVELLES • Roy DUFFIELD • James FITZGIBBON • Michael GIGANDET • J.J. GONZÁLEZ • Jodi Pilcher GORDON • Ken GOSSE • Anne HOWKINS • Mark HUDSON • Barbara Schilling HURWITZ • Nneoma IKE-NJOKU • Doug JACQUIER • Paul JAUREGUI • Pam KNAPP • Eddy KNIGHT • Martha LANDMAN • Tréa LAVERY • Christine LAW • Erica Plouffe LAZURE • Catherine LEE • Joan LEOTTA • Cynthia LESLIE-BOLE • Louella LESTER • Valentina LINARDI • Kirsten LUCKINS • Maduabuchi MacDONALD • Clare MARSH • Jenean McBREARTY • Jan McCARTHY • Rachael MEAD • Barbara A. MEIER • Deborah MELTVEDT • Corey MILLER • Remngton MURPHY • Zach MURPHY • Carl 'Papa' PALMER • Gary PERCESEPE • Christopher PHAM • Sandy PHILLIPS • Melisa QUIGLEY • Emma ROBERTSON • Anna ROSS • Ed RUZICKA • Mir-Yashar SEYEDBAGHERI • Martin SHAW • Jonathan SLUSHER • Robert STEWARD • Crystal STEWART • Andrea TATE • Isabel THOMPSON • Jennifer THRALL • Lucy TYRRELL • Judy UPTON • Lois Perch VILLEMAIRE • Lauren Bronwyn WAGNER • Robert WALTON • Sarah WILLIAMS • Melissa WONG • Larry WRIGHT • Mantz YORKE •

Contents

Poetry

Poetry

Lost on the Coast Road

Rachael Mead

I'm about to get this all wrong. This place,
so stacked with shacks and gin palaces
that I keep getting Middleton and Marion Bay
stuck together in my head, both flecked
and slapped with the Southern Ocean and its winds.
The windows are down and we let
the air overtake as Alistair's car carries us
like a metaphor that doesn't quite work.
The moon is fat with light
and floating in a sneeze of stars
so we crank back the seats and let
the screams of gulls replace conversation.
We've rambled ourselves to a standstill
and Bulkey wants food so we turn east
without a map, as though some Orient exists,
searching for something intangible yet substantial,
spiced with fiery accusations of its own.
I don't venture an opinion but should know better.
We're all equally confident in being lost
and sometimes getting it wrong on a coast road,
the breezy tangle of stars and street lights finding us
then letting us go, is actually getting it right.

Marriage

Gary Percesepe

I

As a wound gives off its own light
I forgive you.
All the lamps of the house are trimmed

against this virus
though it may merely be delayed.
I married again

(you knew that).
But did you know that
she took all my notebooks?

II

It's OK. I don't miss them
or even need them.
You've cut through me

deeper than any stylus.
Besides, it's the same
story over and over

what's broke wasn't glass
what remains can't be hid.
Still, she burned your clothes

on the wide lawn yesterday
the skirt you'd left
the red bra hanging

from the wet curtain.
I make her crazy the
way you made me cry.

III

We're an integrated circuit
a washing machine with
agitator pounding us clean.

I still love you
You make me cry
Two things you'll

never hear again from me.
I'd kill you, she says
But I'd need to make another

just like you. Pain rests,
beauty never. My life
turned and ran down the stairs.

IV

Who is she?
I stammered. Names,
I want names.

There is something so pure
she said, in the first
infidelity of the marriage.

Yes, I said.
Her name? she insisted.
Her, I said.

Isn't that enough?
What would you say
if I knew you'd be lying?

V

When neither are married
it's like the story a
novelist tells

the day Hirohito went on air
and spoke as a mortal man
the adults sat around the radio and cried.

Driving Around

Remngton Murphy

There was always a problem
With Blue Diamond Highway,

Lake Meade Boulevard
And Interstate 15.

They always took him
Where he didn't want to go.

He'd wind up in the desert
Looking at the new developments,

Nice little townhouses
Going for eighty, maybe a hundred thousand,

The kind that were foreclosed
During the subprime mortgage crunch.

Or he'd wind up in the desert,
Swatting the sand flies

Getting in his face,
Counting the ground squirrels

And swatting more sand flies.
Either way he was lost.

Spout about the Roundabouts

Carl 'Papa' Palmer

I found myself astound about,
confound about, profound about
these traffic circle roundabouts.

Without a doubt, shouting out
about our renowned roundabouts.
I found myself astound about,

day in day out, frowned about,
bound to pout, wound about
these traffic circle roundabouts.

Bouts of gout have sprouted out
brought about by roundabouts.
I found myself astound about,

spellbound about, touted out,
expounded out, devout about
these traffic circle roundabouts.

As I scouted out my rounded route,
horns sounded out, resounded out.
I found myself astound about
these traffic circle roundabouts.

Follow Your

Dave Clark

Follow your head.
Rational.
Follow your heart.
Emotional.
Follow your gut.
Instinctual.
Follow your values.
Spiritual.
Follow your dreams.
Hopeful.

Decisions made
And justified
And questioned
And regretted
By what we followed.

At times I give
One approach more weight,
Though I ponder whether it's better
To follow one
Or a mix of all
And what are the right amounts of each.

Internal opinions
Pulling me in varied directions.
I stretch like spandex,
And when snapped back,
I am shaped differently.

The color of glass

John Bost

The color of glass when it breaks
Is shattered, splintered, and scattered
Where no one wants to step
Where no one wants to be
They back away or walk around
Avoiding the many broken pieces
shattered, splintered, and scattered
can be difficult to do
can be difficult to see
when so many avert their eyes
they just may not realize
They back away or walk around
Avoiding the many broken pieces
they can fail to see
The color of glass when it breaks

Regrets

Jan Chronister

When I taught on the reservation
students spilled news every week—
parents, aunties, uncles, cousins,
suicide, overdose, diabetes, heart attack.
Mothers and fathers younger than I was
but most likely wiser, death
an accepted fact of life.

It's been a month since
someone I know died,
mother—in—law buried
six months shy of turning 100.
We left in haste before the casket
was lowered, didn't wait around
to watch her body descend into
Florida's sandy ground,
dirt filled back in. Our minds
were on the trip back home,
beating the snow to Wisconsin.

Next year we will visit her grave,
make amends for our slight.

New shoes

Cathie Aylmer

Old slippers are comfy, cosy, safe;
Memories of childhood Christmases
and watching TV before bedtime.
No risk of trips or twisted ankles,
No chance of blisters or blood,
No broken straps or broken heels.
No concerns about a fashion faux pas,
or where to wear them and try them out:
They fit and are comfy and cosy and safe.

But slippers don't have that thrill,
That first glimpse passing by the shoe store window;
Stopping, stepping forward to get a better look;
transfixed.
So beautiful you can't help yourself,
Giving in to the urge,
A splurge!
A dazzling impulse buy...
Which doesn't really pay off.

Looking longingly through the glass at a pair for weeks,
Detouring to take another peek
At the dark, sensual leather
and the sleek lines
of the spiked heels
that are calling your name.
Picturing elongated legs sashaying by
as every step is envied… then complimented.
A payday purchase that is only likely to lead to pain.

Maybe I should stick with the slippers.
Or go barefoot.
But sometimes,
sometimes you need new shoes.

All Sorrow's a Country—Western Song

Tobie Alfier

One plaid flannel in the threadbare closet.
Pearl snaps buttoned like a door slammed,
keeping out the gnats, the heat,
the humid shoal of fog that loiters.

It was a deadly disagreement,
a payday embarrassment,
all her clothes are gone. You are a stranger
to yourself—how you gonna pass by

the couple next door, still in their honeymoon phase
after fifty years of a bounty of strengths.
You can't even sing the words to whatever
you both did wrong, but you know it was mostly you.

An empty shoebox and some extra old Christmas cards
on the shelf on her side.
Just a bit of dust under the bed. Your car mags
piled lonely on the bookshelf with an empty can

of Fosters from the shithole liquor store
around the corner—a clash with the moth–eaten
green curtains you never got around
to replacing with anything nice.

Don't even turn on the FM. You're an AM guy
one hundred percent. Not the first cowboy
to be wailing about your hurts all day, your letter
of apology mailed, fated to no reply.

Interstate 70

Barbara A. Meier

The milo rusts in the field while above
a hazy light surrounds the blades of a turbine windmill,
creating a nimbus against the forever sky.
The clouds weep on the horizon and I am on their path of tears,
filling memory pools as I drive Interstate 70.

An asphalt time tunnel rumbling
across the prairie, abandoning the farms,
leaving limestone fence posts leaning
with saggy belts of barbwire into the wind,
The pumpjacks bedded in the pastures,
rocking the cattle to sleep.

The grain elevators are mostly crumpled metal
discarded by the train tracks. Not one engine slows
as they barrel across the High Plains, leaving towns
mostly deserted, and buildings boarded.

My Subaru leaves no trace on I–70 as I accelerate,
acknowledging to myself: there's no reason to stay.
Again.
I left then as now, without leaving much of a trace;
a caricature on a wall, some photos in some yearbooks,
and a few memories in some people's minds.

My life could have been different.

In either case I'd still be alone
like the nodding donkeys in the field,
with Kansas and me lost
and forsaken in the rear–view window.

Broken Washer

Chuka Susan Chesney

Rotate your whites
lickety split
after that don't tumble
any more of your outfits

My boyfriend's washer's
broken I have to whoosh
somber hues for him
in the midafternoon

I'm driving back soon
in an hour or two
I want the laundry room
to be vacated then
Can't do it tonight
we're going out for drinks

Two hours later:

Why are you spinning
your confetti colors now?
Don't you remember
my boyfriend's laundry?

No you can't do his loads
that's a hard NO
He doesn't even KNOW you

How would you like it
if someone you didn't KNOW
washed your foul–smelling
nighties and camisoles?

Don't touch his shorts
Now we won't have
laundered sheets

I guess I have an extra
set out in my guesthouse
and they're double
but they're coral

He also has a double
but he prefers navy
or nebulous gray

I suppose
we could sleep on
the lower count weave
I'll return in the morning
Hope you'll be asleep

Love off course

Melissa Wong

Take my love because I don't need it back
You have none for my melancholy heart
So, let me be free and let us now part
Save the idea of love under attack
Let me find a love that has what ours lacks
Because we went the wrong way from the start
Finger–painted over what could've been great art
And now, it's time to paint this eyesore black.

Speed of Light

Sarah Williams

It has taken me thirteen years to read this book.
How many lives lived since then?
How many oceans crossed, babies born,
hearts broken and healed?

You, too, once held this book in your hands.
Hands that first touched mine on a cold November night
as the dark sky burst into a thousand stars above the River Mersey
the tang of cheap gunpowder
catching at the back of our throats.

I inhale
like a coke fiend
enjoying one last hit,
hoping to find a sliver of you
between its yellowed pages.

Senses defeated,
time refuses to rewind
when all I smell
is a musty old book,
sitting on the shelf
too long.

Endings

Angelo Auciello

I don't do endings very well
and   beginnings get most of the attention
the Weekly, Cleo, Cosmo
all agree—
most of the fun's there.

In the musty, empty classroom
at the end of the day
I am surprised none even ask:
When do we stop breathing
into the mouth of the person
lying prostrate before us?

Once begun, you must continue,
wide–bottomed, big boned instructor
eyeing pretty, freshly minted
female teacher   replies.

Gradual destinations   I have always preferred
non–botoxed Venice to St Petersburg.
Yes   *do not go gentle*
but in the end   it's the
only way to go   at least
it's what I've always thought.

What if there's no end in sight?

Replies the instructor of the wide X—pants
still fancying his chances:
it's the law, care of duty demands it
once embarked…

> *They who put their hand to the plough*
> *and keep looking back…*
> *He remembers something from*
> *Sunday school years—*
> *John the Baptist*
> *giving him and all unrepentant Pharisees*
> *short shrift.*

Is the spirit still willing even
as the flesh lies limp.

Remember   breathes wide boy
into open—minded young teacher's face
panting to un—finish something:
air exhaled has five percent less oxygen
than air inhaled

What if he's dead? I half rise out of my chair.
What if she's dead?

Big boned hopeful looks at me—
for the first time:
You won't be the one to know that
your two breaths are now one.

Clan House

Larry Wright

Fish and rice
That was the smell that hit me
As we passed through the front door.
It could be yesterday or tomorrow
Or what I remember from 45 years ago
And yet that familiar smell that speaks
Of common homes and conditions
Remains fresh in my mind.
Grandma's house bent more towards
Potato dumplings, venison stew and fresh baked bread.
But here it was the fish
Which my mind could not separate from the rice.
Salmon steaks and baked salmon
Deep−fried halibut and herring eggs in oil
And always accompanied by rice.
In that house, at that time, and still, the homely perfume
Permeated the finely crocheted covers on the armchairs
And the credenza covered with old pictures
Small medals and trophies all arranged atop the fine
White lace like eggs in a nest.
Eggs that smelled like fish and rice.

The house had history. It represented something.
The house has history. It still represents.
But I didn't know that then and I barely know now.
A house full of stoic faces and mute mementos
Wrapped in somber regard and slow time
And I missed almost all of it then
Because I didn't know the spirits
Who were there with me
Because I didn't know
This house stretched back through time
Thousands of years, taking my blood into the past.
How different life might have been
If I had stopped then, in that house
Stepped out of my own quiet and listened to those spirits
And spoke with them
About time, and blood
And the future.

My biggest regrets from my Wisconsin vacation

Mark Hudson

My two biggest regrets from my vacation to Wisconsin were:

A: We saw a fake airplane that was sticking out of some bushes in the middle of a country road on the side of the road, (or perhaps it was a real plane) with the tail sticking up in the air. I regret not taking a picture with it.

B: My second biggest regret is that we went to a county fair, and we didn't stay long, but they had a place where you could get your picture taken with a monkey, but we left. I already have a picture of me with a snake from Reptile Fest in Chicago, but the monkey picture would've been good too.

Sunday, 10 Degrees Fahrenheit

Kersten Christianson

When Fiona Ritchie spins "Neil Gow's Lament
for His Second Wife" every third Sunday

on *Thistle & Shamrock*, I'm transplanted
back to summers ticking off the kilometers

of the Trans–Canada Highway in a Ford Ranger
pickup; your left hand on the wheel, your right

on my thigh. Flame of lupine chase us
to another ocean. You laugh at my French

and we live by tent, campfire and Double–Doubles
from Tim Hortons. Now, you gone too soon,

I don't know how to continue this as my forever,
except through words. So, I skirt the soft shoulder

of recollection and heart; these words both light
dust and heavy stone.

That Flicker of Perfection

Dev Berger

So many things went wrong.
The first kiss with the
wrong person.
The last kiss with the
right person whose words
of love were buried
in the grave,
that I could not pull
through the soil,
and those clouds that fell
into the ocean
that I had no time
to photograph.

Why is it always
so easy to identify
what is wrong,
but so hard to capture
that flicker of perfection?
And why can't we remember
the importance of looking
behind shadows,

or memorize
how the sunlight
slants against
the meadows?

Why is it impossible
to reproduce
the electricity streaming through
fingers a loved one holds
against our skin,
and why
can't we duplicate
the messages
from a racing pulse that
screams the truths
created by the whisper
of a loved one's scent?

The chapter of our lives
where the smudges
of sweet nothings
leave behind
the imprints of so
many things that went right.
And yet ...
Why is it so hard to remember
the things that
did not go wrong?

Heavy Load

Kirsten Luckins

Sometimes I am a dead seed
rattled by griefs. Then
I am a bridge in high winds,
hawsers plucked. Tremors
thread my innards.

Did I seem braided steel to you?
Be honest, did I ever strike you as load—bearing?
These and other high—sided questions
slew across both lanes.
Will we ever have a leader who loves us?
Are they really eating rats in Caracas?

M&S are trying to sell me stew as a superfood.
Lloyds will give me what my GP won't, but
fees apply.
Should I tell the pharmacy guy?
About the thing that lurches
through the back of my head?
I wave lists, I dangle podcasts.

Insufficient.

The Eater of Hope on its hundred ickle feet

is making slurry of my chocolate–coated me–time.

It wants it wants it wants to know

answers to questions more shameful than these.

Brittle

Lisa Collyer

If I could take back— then I would
scrape tongue of bitter words
that blister heart on impact.

Take acrid words— spit them back,
burn lips & make them seep
a caustic, gore drip.

It's not true what I said,
save that I said it.
Spite told— I love you
for mere want, of want to hurt.

I am inept at most things
except hurt, hurt I get fat on.
If I could wash out acid pit
— then I would.

Ifs

Maduabuchi MacDonald

It's vivid… the denials of my established principles
subways of tears hug my face like tree bark
The words "it's just this once" had planted my deep downfall
I can see my shame beside the cemetery I stand

It was going to be the last time I gifted the driver Drink in the car
And it was the last time I saw Dad mount his car
The last tune I danced for death
And as a debutant, he grabbed his last minute goal

If only stinginess had befriended me
And I had heeded my established principles
And hugged discipline like a daughter welcoming her mum
If only… There were no 'ifs'

The Devil Takes
The Could–a–beens

Doug Jacquier

Beware the wine–sodden brain flailing on,
kidding itself in the darker hours,
paying homage to could–a–been.
Beware the anger trotted out,
dusted off and laid bare to reflections in a bloodshot eye,
to spring a self–laid trap.
Let there be a new start,
urged on by forebodings of irrelevance
and eternity horizontal.
Stay away from old ground,
where every night is New Year's Eve and nothing is resolved,
or risk seeing past comrades on distant hills,
their torch–dreams kindled by motion,
pausing less and less often to look back
at your immobile figure.
Standing still,
the grubby sticks of history are consumed quickly
in those parodies of hell,
the warmthless braziers of bitter reminiscence.

Forsake all wretchedness,
for you are not plundered.
Beneath your public rags lie priceless jewels,
secreted and perversely forgotten,
whose re-discovery waits on nakedness.
Choose not to wear sackcloth
and arise from your meal of ashes,
hungry for the flesh of the world
and the hard beauty of your diamond self.

Yellow Bus

Lucy Tyrrell

Beyond the silver chain link fence,
old yellow buses wait
at 3 pm when school is out—
kids wriggle into lines.

When all the drivers nod and call,
closed gates are opened wide
and noisy children clamber on
the buses at each stall.

Steel gates are numbered one to nine
for routes to take us home.
My bus is Number 2, I know—
it goes down Kennett Pike.

For reasons I forget right now,
I leave the classroom late,
so when I rush from school to gate,
the bus is backing out.

I open latch and run on through—
determined, that's for sure—
to catch that backing bus before
it strands me there alone.

The shout I hear is shrill and loud,
more steel in voice than fence—
"Come back, come back—don't run out there—
you're not allowed to go."

Though teacher stopped the bus back then,
her yelling crosses years—
in innocence I fought back tears
on yellow bus ride home.

Over a Lifetime

Sandy Phillips

Back in my childhood
where many regrets began,
I saw only me and me.

Never realised how much I owed my mother who
had a very hard life. She could have given me up
and made it easier for herself, as an unwed mother.
What would she say if I asked now?

Early twenties
brought many wrong decisions, in my doom and gloom years
even my children didn't get the love and attention they
deserved. But the ultimate loser was me.
Missing out on all that joy.

Further on up the line
My decisions were wiser,
less likely to be regretted later.
However long that may be.

Memories, sweet and not so sweet, only result in weeping,
Wishing them away will not work, so what's to be done?
Nothing, except to appeal to a higher court for judgement,
Ask for forgiveness at the gates
And release from these memories
Or try to forgive myself,
Ah! That is the hardest job of all.

My Past

Valentina Linardi

If turning back
isn't that bad
then why
pray tell, why
do we run from the past like this?
Any chance I get
I run in fear
of what I know already.
What's worse
than what I know already?
I was given this chance
and I'm so horrified
so afraid of the past
I felt my anxiety resurfacing
and my heart rate
hasn't been this bad since then
and I ask you
not to judge me
while I run away
saying it's not your fault
– my past, know
it's not your fault.

I'm used to looking forward
telling myself
anywhere is better than my past.

The present is quick to disappoint me.

I'm quick to disappoint me.

Chu Chi Tunnels

Melisa Quigley

I climbed down
Hurriedly into a tunnel
Squatting, crawling
Dirt under my feet
Earthy smell
Blocks my nostrils
Stifled to breathe
Regretting not
Taking my asthma medication
Trying to think of
Pleasant things
People in front of me
People behind
Stopping, moving forward
Torchlight
To guide
Reaching a cross—section
People converge
Someone yells out
'Dead end this way
Go back, turn around'

My heart beats faster
Perspiration streams
Down my legs and face
I want to run
To get out of this place
But turn around slowly
Bumping into
The person behind
And in front
Hands clawing the dirt
Breathing in
Breathing out
With a wheeze
Moving forward
Smiling when
I see the light
Legs shaking
As I climb up
The stairs
Glad to breathe
Fresh air

She Follows Her Heart

Catherine Lee

Consider the pale soul sister who finds herself attracting black.
Her parents hate dark generations.
Her parents' neighbors cannot live that close.
Her black men, so fine, in the moment satisfy
until commitments go to other loves.

She follows her heart

Black sisters see the color of competition, name her becky
say she has no right to ruin families.
So many communities cut her out.

Consider the pale soul sister. She spends so much time alone
accumulating proofs of African descent.
Who but a soul sister can tell of losing a man to silence
hearing less from a best girlfriend
finding   eventually   both of them at once

A pale soul sister stays lifelong friends with her
and follows heartfelt urging
not to speak the word betrayal   more times than once.
She learns   so slowly.   She keeps trying.

She follows her heart

More recently her men: musicians
always on the road maintaining separate residences.
They make her feel good.
They sometimes hang with her when they're in town.
They come, rejecting the proffered permanence
while not exactly rejecting her advances.
They leave her sleepless with hunger
speechless with remorse when they go.

Mrs M.

Tony Daly

My first patient
Said she wouldn't eat
unless I fed her

I'd set her tray
in front of her and
ask how she was
She'd push herself up
on her elbows and
talk about her
lost youth while
spooning soft food
to parchment lips

No one missed the
clinical student, so
I lent her my time
listened to her life

She had been
    beautiful
    dancer
    soldier's wife
    mother
    Riveting Rosie
    college graduate
She was proud of her life
I was inspired

She called me "Saint"

She died this morning—alone
before my shift started

She's the last patient
whose name I remember

At the Spanish Steps in the Softness of May

Martha Landman

My eyes are drawn
to a man sprinting up the stairs
Piazza di Spagna
his sleeveless sweatshirt
pale yellow as a crescent moon
soft–running shoes —
in blue, mind you!
He could be
        Italian, Portuguese
           the Spanish sailor
               I met three decades ago.

His head bobs through the crowd
his greying ponytail follows
on intermittent stops for photo shoots —
        the longboat fountain,
        Roman hills,
           the Holy See below.

Forza on his inner arm,
could be a lover's name
or saying he's still a powerhouse.
In full view I snap him,

      once,

           twice,

                even a third time.

And then he's gone. Weeks later
I google, discover Keats' house, now a museum,
is at the bottom of those stairs —

           and I regret

Leaving the Solomons

Deborah Meltvedt

You asked about the Peace Corps
What happened?
I said I remember tasting mangoes for the
very first time. The milk came from
coconuts I sucked from a straw like
Mary Ann on *Gilligan's Island.*

But what happened?
I said the geckos were scattered
all over the walls and the heat
was a blanket you couldn't throw down
and we spoke Pidgin English
me likem one—fala Fosters
when I ordered a beer.

But what really happened?
Do you want to hear about a child's
swollen belly or the Betel Nut—juiced lips of their mothers?
The common spray of insecticide that emptied city streets
or the sharp cuts of shell beaches?

I couldn't tell you the reason I
went was the same reason
I left. Silly white girl from Fresno
wanting *to do something good*
to make up for not being good
at bodies or boyfriends or math or
being Daddy's little girl,
so instead
I would save the world.

How do I explain how I left in thirty days, not two years?
The island's nectar bubbled my throat, the milk turned sour and
the ghosts of good intentions told me
to go back, fly 3000 miles
to a yellow–tiled kitchen, to slicing bananas on corn flakes and biting
fat delicious apples on an autumn day.

How do I tell you about the bruised fruit of shame?

You asked about the Peace Corps.
I told you I remember tasting mangoes for the very first time.

In the public interest

Anne Casey

A single blue−black blot floats in an eggshell sky
as I pull the blinds, eyes catching a russet streak
disappearing into the scrub. Outlaw into outlaw—
a lone fox vanishing into condemned bushland—
our precious reserve exempt from protection,
over−ridden by State law provisions: to *provide*
for the burgeoning urban population, a new tunnel
which (for unclear reasons) will exclude public transport.

A single blue−black blot floats on my eggshell
shoulder after cries in the blue−black night,
waking to the clatter and bang—storming
uniforms, blue−black in the harsh flash
of overhead fluorescents, prodded by
rifle−butts from crowded bunks: *Papers, papers!*
Recognising machine−guns without knowing how
or why, I fear the need for small white lies.

A single blue–black blot floats in my eggshell
palm as I give the well–rehearsed answer,
my non–birthright passport held until
my occupation is cross–checked, passes muster.
Communications worker and I am waved on
into the waiting throng. Another barrier crossed,
knowing just by owning my work, I can be
deemed wrong, on my return to *safer* soil.

A single blue–black blot floats on an eggshell form:
this small seal of *approval* as my counterpart pulls
the blinds, to view the warrant—privacy disappearing
into thin air: a lone trust, long–held, vanishing in this dawn
police raid on rights to know, investigate, report—privileges
over–ridden, withheld by sweeping new federal laws:
domicile overturned for reporting on secret talks
to probe our text messages, emails, bank records.

A single blue–black blot blinks in the eggshell sky—
as we pull the blinds—invisible to the naked eye.

Note:
On 4 June 2019, Australian Federal Police—acting on a warrant granted
under the auspices of protecting Australia's national security—raided the
home of a journalist who had investigated a leaked plan to allow widespread
new government powers to spy on Australian citizens.
On 1 July 2020, China passed a new national security law, bringing
uncertainty for freedom of the press and broader civilian rights in Hong
Kong.

Passion Plays

James Bell

After the painting City and Night and Music *by Maciej Ciesia*

the way she lays her head
on his shoulder

as he plays the clarinet
a slow number a woman sways against

in tenderness
most heads lean as if

they too seek a shoulder
some touch

to cross the border
between sound and vision

the double bass bends in to
embrace his instrument

strokes its strings intuitively
in this jazz quartet

around the piano for company
with their improvised notes of old regrets

the lights still bright
yet they won't stop playing until dawn

then might leave this parallel world
find the need to travel

much further on this journey
as they and their audience stay where they are

Regret from Above

Lauren Bronwyn Wagner

I sat on top of the world
Grasping at souls to release the hurt
While shadows danced and divvied up our time
I lost control of yours, before it became mine
You faltered, you floundered
You dissolved a mountain of lies
I sat watching, but you did not look at me this time

I sat on top of the world
Experiencing unmeasurable hurt
While you played the jester one step out of time
I gave you back yours, before you could take mine
You flourished, you favoured
You absolved every handwritten rhyme
I sat, unable to conjure up another single line
Because you couldn't see me this time

I sat on top of the world
Not quite as sacred as all the other girls
While you romanced the whole of humankind
They gave you theirs, but you still didn't have mine
You fancied, you fascinated
You forebode anyone wanting to shine
I sat, glistening – as you turned your head to the side...

...You saw me the moment before our worlds were to collide

But I slipped away, and you hold regret inside

Global Warming,
You Bet Ya!

Ed Ruzicka

We got a Nasty norther frying asphalt here.
A scorch of dry wind flat–slaps my cheek.
No one expected this at Mardi Gras.
Least of all the frilly Azalea blooms that
flounce their skirts up and down the street
then fall out brown on dried grass.

Punishing. I can almost hear the birds
curse in their branches. Look at how
the homeless stagger slow behind shop–carts
restless under layers, baked.

Nobody wants this. Least of all the men
who cling one hand gripped to a bar at a truck back
while the other arm flails like a bronc–breaker's.
Garbage trucks have exoskeletons harder
than grub beetle shells. They rumble
and quake around the neighborhood in patterns
determined as a grub beetle's paths.

This is a real gut—wrencher, this one —
like a tapeworm is working me from the inside out.
Maybe a few slugs of strong Joe could solve it,
edge it off —cause that's the only remedy
for some mornings. How's your f ing life?

One Step Beyond the Final Frontier

Ken Gosse

A Flat Earth explorer sailed every deep ocean,
for seeking Earth's Edge was his lifelong devotion.
In calm or in storm,
he encountered one norm—
either sand or hard land broke the sea's endless motion.

A Flat Earth explorer reached Everest's great height
in his search for the Edge, one more step in his plight,
but up at the top
there was no sudden drop—
only mountains beyond, with no ending in sight.

A Flat Earth explorer, in thirst and great pain
crawled across endless deserts, but always in vain
for each hot grain of sand
thwarted all that he planned—
and his failure burned deeply, while frying his brain.

A Flat Earth explorer o'er vast prairies flew
in a high–masted wagon, both captain and crew,
'til one day it was plain
this was also in vain—
snow–capped peaks without end extend beyond view.

A Flat Earth explorer in China one night
found the edge of the Earth, which he climbed in delight!
He scaled a Great Wall
knowing soon he would fall ...
At the top, more horizons—his efforts' worst blight.

A Flat Earth explorer, as brave as can be,
traversed the Antarctic without company
when he felt a great quake
and he saw the edge break—
peering over, he saw only icebergs at sea.

A Flat Earth explorer made one final pledge
to continue his search from a great flying sledge
tied beneath a balloon
which he took to the Moon.
"One small step for a man ..." sent him over the edge.

Evergreen

Crystal Stewart

Turn your back on the evergreens
Traipse through the golden leaves
As you forge forward
Tiny spines snap underfoot
Do they feel resistance
As they melt into winter
Do their crimson bodies feel pain
Or do they embrace the cycle of life
Spring will heal over with its youth again.

The scarred boughs of this tree
have made a pact with the seasons
The soft April rain will
Remind you of its journey
Each bud biding its time
From famine to plenty.

Nature never mourns each passing
Rings drawn through an ageing heart
Expand with love, not regret.

Turn and Return

Charles N. deGravelles

For Mike Palmintier

Lay the saw on its side and leave the room
   as it is, half–finished. Sawdust will settle

its own affairs. Once you give it a good
   pull, the story, like the loose thread, keeps

on coming.... "The contract was never written
   that contemplates all the ways we can

hurt each other....." Nor will the knitting ever
   end. Therefore, lift fingers from piano keys,

computer keys. Let the insouciant laundry dry
   on the line. Disentangle, turn it loose, sit

down for a single moment and close your eyes. Consider
   who you think you are not, then, having pulled

yourself clean out of context (circumstances
   you were always confident constituted your life)

consider again....

A delay on the line

Roy Duffield

Dear little brother,

I've been wanting to write to you
For a while now.
I want you to know
You'll be able
To ride it out.
That even though
Through the smoke
You can't see it yet
There's light at the end of the tunnel
Plenty more tunnels
And plenty more lights ahead
Don't forget our time—capsule
We buried in the ground.
I could really do with it
More than ever, now.
I'll try to dig it up
If I ever come around.
You'll get out of there too, kid
In the end.

Yours always,
Your brother and your friend

Hey big brother!

It was nice to get your note.
I hope while you're driving,
You won't pick up the phone.
Don't get lost
In the memories.
Keep your eyes on the road.
Don't ever turn back and come back for us.
You know you're better off alone.
When I grow up, I hope I'm like you.
I love you,
You know.
But don't talk about the future,
Or my present,
Yet.
Just let me stay another day,
Buried,
In my bed.

Last Summer

Tréa Lavery

Last summer
I bought a film camera at a yard sale
Along with five rolls of film
That expired before the new millennium.
It cost me two dollars for the set
And twenty−six to get the first roll developed,
Having the drugstore ship it off
To who−knows−where
So Kodak could work their magic.

I told you that expired film was a "thing"
That people used it to create
A "vintage aesthetic"
As if to remind themselves of the passage of time.
You thought it was a waste of two dollars
So I didn't tell you how expensive it is
To get film developed.

The pictures came out awful.
I don't know if the film was just too far gone
Or if the point−and−shoot ruined my shots
But it wasn't a "vintage aesthetic,"
It was just a mess.

I still have the other four rolls of film,
As if those might take back in time
In the same way the first one
Didn't.
What a waste of twenty−eight dollars
And a waste of a summer day.

Pool Decked

Robert Walton

You're fired, kid.

But these bus carts are decrepit!
The wheels stick
On every little bump
And that pool deck is all bumps.
I know where they are now!
I'll go slower next time.

Slower, right.

Much slower —
It was crowded, too —
A girl stepped in front of me,
The one in the yellow bikini.

Yellow bikini, right.

And I got it all cleaned up!
Fast!
Besides, the snack bar didn't need
Five whole gallons of
Thousand Island!

You're fired.

Prose

Prose

Not going back

Clare Marsh

9 April 2020

Dear Nikolai, Dmitry and Steven,

We, the crew members of Expedition 62, would like to welcome you aboard for mission handover—but can't. We hope you guys can read this letter through the porthole and understand our decision. In our position we think you'd probably do the same.

Life on earth has changed fundamentally in the 200+ days since we left and we have no wish to return to a world ravaged by pandemic. We're safe here and the view is unique, seeing our amazing planet in a new light as pollution diminishes. We can carry on doing science up here, so no need for us to feel guilty.

Sorry that the hatch between our Poisk service module and your Soyuz MS−16 spacecraft won't be opened on the ISS side after docking. Mission Control will just have to accept we are staying put. They may think we're 'going rogue', but it's not like they can nip up here to drag us back, is it? While we won't get the supplies you've brought, we've been rationing ours since the start of the year when all this kicked off. There are always the emergency reserves to dip into and we can stay in virtual contact with our families—just as we would if 'socially distancing' back home.

Sorry you've had a wasted journey, but we hope you enjoyed your six—hour flight and four orbits of the earth. Have a great ride back down to Kazakhstan!

All the best
Ivan, Madison and James.

Threadbare

Bethany Cody

The woman in room thirteen says he smells. She can blame
Mick all she wants but it won't change the fact the water here is
bad – tepid, coming out of calcified showerheads in irregular
spurts if the pressure is high and if not, it's an undignified
dribble like Mick's grandpa used to make in his underwear each
time the old man sat down to chain–smoke in front of the TV.
In spite of the pipes Mick likes the place enough to stay. It's
been about a year now.

There's a whole lot of it out here, this place built smack–
bang in the middle of silent nothing, dirt, flat earth, skeletal
shrubs hollowed out by wind and fried within an inch of life by
an unconcerned sun. No trees, no river, no town closer than
twelve hundred kilometres. Big Sky country if you're looking
up and out instead of down at the clouds of dust your shoes
kick up walking over woefully waterless ground, avoiding
snakes and scorpions.

The sun turns Mick pink like a baby mole and just as ugly,
puts a dozen more dots across his nose and hollow cheeks. His
back is ravaged by them, a thousand needlepoint spots like
mould spores on the ceiling of his dank bathroom. Most are
freckles, some are pimples, others are bites from nocturnal bugs
that make a home between his bedsheets. They don't hurt

unless he picks at them and they get infected. He doesn't mind them.

Somewhere along the way he runs out of money and the guy who owns the place knocks on Mick's door. He stands outside of the half–open doorway while his sweaty, spotty tenant mumbles excuses. He gives Mick a small baggie of drugs to distribute to the other guests and after Mick honours their unspoken agreement, never bothers him again. So the room is Mick's since he checks in, since the woman next–door checks out, cuts her wrist in the bathtub and makes a real mess, since the pair of young idiots in room eight syphon fuel from Mick's tank. He finds out a week later when he gets the itch to take a drive. It gets him hot for all of a minute before he realises there isn't anywhere he has to go. Walking through the Nothing some afternoons, he forges his own path forward on foot.

He helps himself to wafers of soap, coffee sachets, sugar, tea bags on a string, clean towels from vacant rooms left unlocked, to the vending machine making strange music in the front office. There's milk in the fridge and a makeshift pantry with crackers, bread, dehydrated mango strips like sweet jerky from up north. The owner brings supplies every week and in their unspoken agreement or perhaps apathy, absentmindedness, Mick takes from them, shuffles through the motel's empty rooms for necessities, a fleeting cure for listlessness.

It's not always quiet. Noise comes from loved up couples in the room furthest from the office. Mick hears their arguments, apologies, hears the families with young children, university students, the occasional truckie who gets lost, turned around and parks his cargo by the side of the motel like they think the meagre amount of shade will protect against the Burn. Surprise subsides and routine settles in. So used to the monotony of this out—of—the—way place, the arrival of the Newcomer catches Mick off guard.

A man turns up at night. Reverberation from a growling motor calls to something in Mick. He leaves his threadbare mattress to watch from the window. Night is dark beyond, a funerary shroud that haunts everything light from the moon touches, the stars are supernovas. The man parks his car across from Mick's. A cigarette illuminates a focused spotlight on the man's face where Mick finds a greying beard and fatigue. There's a brief intensity to the glow before the cigarette is snuffed out and Mick retreats.

In the morning he visits the vending machine. He learnt if you push a button and rattle the box a little it gives up the goods free of charge. Half—blind and hungry he bumps into the Newcomer. They both want the chocolate bar, the one with vanilla wafers and caramel. Their fingers touch on the stained keypad. A moment of pause passes and the Newcomer laughs, smells like smoke on each exhale.

"Sorry, man. You go first."

Tobacco tang unsettles Mick's stomach and he leaves without a word. Four weeks the guy sticks around, poking holes in Mick's habits, appearing in places Mick likes to think are his own. In the beginning he's subtle about telling the man he stinks, offering him a mint here and there, a stick of gum, tries to stand up—wind when they take a walk through the Nothing in companionable silence. When the man finally catches on, when he notices the wrinkling of Mick's nose, he says, "You don't exactly smell like flowers either, man."

Their cheeks redden like the earth and for the first time in years Mick feels embarrassed for himself. He sees the pit of Mick's stomach, bony speckled arms hanging loose by his sides, colourless tiger—stripes of ribs there too. It's too hot to cover up, to hide scars blemishing the curve of his hips, the hollow of his elbows and forearms.

Mick says, "I think I've done something so bad the stink's on my soul."

He doesn't like to remember why he first came to the motel, doesn't like the names he calls himself when he refuses to leave, setting off memories – bad men, bad things, bodies.

The Newcomer sighs softly. He says, "We've all done things we regret." His wrist turns minutely in the sunlight to taunt tendrils of faded green ink.

Mick's had run—ins with the symbol before. He considers the sparkling sand at their shoes, the pair of black sandals he's wearing, all but collapsed around his feet, the rubber sole so worn through there's holes where his toes come to rest.

"Yeah."

Shrinking Violet

Sandra Arnold

They say children retain no memory of their early years. Not true. Vi has clear memories of lying in her mother's arms swaddled in a blanket, her father standing in the doorway, his eyes pleading for the only answer he wanted to hear. She has clear memories of her mother shaking her head, her father's smile turning upside down and the light dying in his eyes. She has clear memories of herself playing with a doll in a corner of the kitchen, hearing her mother tell her father that the doctor said there would be no more, so Violet was all he was going to get.

She has clear memories of her father whacking her across the face and making her nose bleed when she was five because she wouldn't stop screaming when she saw him drowning her cat's newborn kittens. She was glad the cat ran away after that.

She has clear memories of not answering questions at school because of what might happen if she gave the wrong answer. When teachers looked at her she made herself invisible by closing her eyes and shrinking. Mostly the teachers ignored her when she did this, but one made a point of saying, 'You're too stupid to know the answer so I won't bother waiting for one.'

Her mother asked her why the other children didn't play with her, adding, 'When I was your age I had lots of friends.' Vi didn't know how to explain that she made herself invisible in the playground so she could count the spots on ladybirds' wings. She wished she could be invisible at home too when she was the target of her father's snarls. Only once did she ask her mother why he carried on like this.

Her mother replied, 'The name he wanted was Kevin.'

'But that's not a girl's name,' Vi said.

'No. It isn't,' her mother said.

After that Vi spent most of her time in her room reading books she borrowed from the library.

To everyone's surprise she passed the entrance exam for university. Her chosen subject was philosophy because she wanted to learn how the world worked. She assumed from the beginning that the other students wouldn't see her and she was accurate in that assessment. However, being invisible had its advantages as she could observe the students' facial expressions and social interactions as they walked around the campus and into lecture theatres. Vi practiced these in front of a mirror in her bedroom so she would know what to do in job interviews.

On her first visit back home at the end of term, her father asked her what she'd been studying. When she started to tell him he interrupted and said there was only right and wrong as laid down in the Bible and no shades of grey. Despite her mother's warning Vi told him he was wrong and, predictably, he reminded her that she was a girl and therefore knew nothing about anything. This time she walked out of the room and when he came after her she barricaded herself in the bathroom which was the only room in the house with a lock, ignoring his fists pounding the door and his cursing lifting the roof until her mother pleaded with him to come away before the neighbours heard. Later, when he was asleep, she crept downstairs for something to eat and found her mother weeping. She said, 'When you're at university there's never any trouble. It's only when you're here that he starts.' Vi decided to fix that problem by never going home again.

After graduation she found a job in a library in another city. Each day she closed her eyes and inhaled the smell of books as she shelved them. She began to believe there was a place for her here. Until, in a coffee break, she overheard one of the librarians say to another one, 'She has the kind of face that's devoid of expression. And she doesn't speak unless she's spoken to. How on earth did she get through the interview?'

Vi finished her coffee, collected her coat and left.

She found another job stacking shelves in a small country supermarket. Each night she let herself into the building, switched on the lights and began unpacking the boxes and stacking the shelves. When she was finished, she liked walking around checking each orderly aisle before letting herself out and locking up and biking back to her flat in time to see the sun rise over the hills and the sky turn from grey to gold.

After three months she phoned her parents to tell them she was happy, that she loved biking to work at night when the streets were dark and quiet and she could look at the moon and stars and feel the cold night air on her face and listen to the wind in the trees and witness the swoop of owls. There was a moment's silence. Her father laughed. He said he always knew she'd finish up in some dead—end job. And the phone went dead.

Then one day a virus struck the whole world and the country went into lockdown. The shelves of toilet paper, flour and eggs and bread and baked beans and coffee and tea emptied faster than Vi could replenish them. She started coming to work an hour earlier and leaving an hour later to get the job done.

After her longest shift in a month the delivery van dropped bundles of newspapers at the door. She picked them up as usual to place them by the check—out counters and saw the front page was full of photographs. As she looked more closely she saw they were photographs of street cleaners, road workers, rubbish collectors and supermarket shelf stackers. The headline read **INVISIBLE HEROES.** Vi slid a copy into her bag.

Counseling

Mir-Yashar Seyedbagheri

Go see a counselor, classmates pronounce, when I ask for company. Friendship.

"It'll help," the ringleader of the pro-counseling legion proclaims. Her name is Betty Brown, she wears huge glasses, and I suspect she has a few glaring issues of her own. "It'll help you get balance. You'll find peace in your life, Nick."

Balanced? What the fuck? I want a friend. I want a real friend.

As if counselors can compensate for the vast spaces between me and people, the empty rooms at night, the excessive time spent with Netflix and its soothing red glow. Can counselors make people respond to the emails I send? Are they punishing me for bluntness unmasked? Counselors are just as messed up, truth be told. They're people who disguise sorrows beneath diagnoses and cold recommendations. Take this pill. Oh wait, the counselors haven't become full-fledged psychiatrists yet. Get more exercise.

I'd like a friend. That's what every email I send states. Have coffee or beer with me. Come over to my place, watch *The Big Lebowski*, smoke a joint. Things friends do. That's the truth. No frills, no power games.

I need a friend. I need a friend. That phrase also peppers electronic screens when *like* doesn't do the trick. I don't even get a fleeting promise of coffee or beer, a promise to talk. Just ignorance and counseling recommendations.

"It'll make you whole," Betty says of counseling, as if I'm an egg.

The only thing I have in common with an egg is we're cracked.

To Betty and cohorts, counseling is supposed to be the magical answer. Counseling is supposed to wash away the disgust they wear when I approach them, their condescension when they explain their philosophies about life, writing, everything. It's all about simple diagnosis, a couple pills, and an upbeat attitude, or the semblance thereof. Does it work for Betty? She walks a little too fast, laughs a tad too loud. What's she hiding?

I grew up the son of a mendicant father. He expected me to inherit the title of mendicant, who moved among their own friends with cold calculation and threw them under the bus with great aplomb. Doublespeak pervaded parties. Smiles concealed backstabbing and private jokes. I thought grad school would be different, a place where people could check the power games.

I wish my classmates would just tell me what their problem is. Is it that I'm blunt? That I'm a neo—Romantic, tapping into untrammeled emotion? Or is it that I don't write about people pulverized by trains and perpetually popping pills?

I guess it's easier for them to live in subtexts and lies. Meanwhile, I live in dark rooms and concrete quads, people passing so fast, an energy that's frenetic.

My classmates live for the art of transactions, gathering in their own circles, at the bar after workshop, at readings. They pontificate about writing, fawn before professors. The teachers are pipelines to publishers and other teaching positions. Once they leave the classroom, they disparage the professors as bourgeois bastards in berets. I catch snatches of conversation down the halls and in the quad.

I shouldn't bother them. But they're the only people I know.

I imagine personal communion at the bar or in a restaurant, a convergence of bodies. I imagine sharing my own secrets with them, confessing my hope for a life that isn't transactional and predicated on bullshit. I imagine classmates who let me in on their jokes, so seemingly elusive. I imagine my laughter rising like the breeze on a spring night. I imagine so much, I imagine in dreams, I wake up in tears.

Some nights, I walk by the little frame houses where they're holding their parties with lit windows, chipped yellow paint, and old−school charm. I watch my classmates moving with grace, carrying cartons of beer, envy their lives rife with possibility. I think of just slipping in but can never find the nerve. What would they do? Throw me out? More likely relegate me to a corner, like a leper at a hockey game. I just walk up and down the street, like an innocent pedestrian, inhale snatches of laughter and pot smoke and Lady Gaga blasting from speakers that thump. Thump, thump, thump, a pleasing beat. A beat I could dance to, moving about charming small rooms and basements.

I keep emailing. I tell them I really need company. I feel shame, but what else do I do? I imagine suppressing everything. Imagine the hateful person I'd become, imagine myself telling someone else to get counseling.

They ignore me. They talk over me in the computer lab, look past me in the English department halls, and dart around me in the courtyards. Betty mentions counseling again while they chatter about more parties and gatherings. They just talk of who's coming and who they want to come and how they hope to get this big-name writer to crash. They quote Tolstoy, distort him, and keep on planning.

For a time, I drop F—bombs into my speech, make proclamations. But my walk wobbles, my smile dissolves. Classmates ask if I have a physical disability and I swallow a laugh. I'm Frankenstein's monster, a mélange of others' expectations. Shame tugs at me.

I refresh emails. I keep waiting, waiting, trying to figure out how to express myself.

I tell myself to stand firm. But even the firmest souls sink into surrender.

The Stepfather

Michael Gigandet

"You're holding the world's knowledge in your hands, every smack dab of it," the college boy in a cheap suit with the Mercury 7 astronaut haircut said.

My stepfather looked at the encyclopedia and caressed the cover as if he were smoothing out a wrinkle, a sure sign to me that he was going to buy something else we couldn't afford, but astronaut boy did not know that.

"And I'm gonna give you my family discount too," he said. "Not supposed to, but I'm gonna anyway."

Not only did my stepfather buy 26 volumes of "Knowledge of the World" Encyclopedias with the two-volume index, he ordered the 24 volumes of "People of the World". He even bought the wooden bookshelf that came with them.

You could sell the man anything. That's how my mother sold him marriage to a woman with three children.

"You kids won't have an excuse not to do your home-work," my stepfather said, smiling, pleased with himself, justifying this extravagance and joking at the same time. He'd never completed high school, so I guess he had reason to be impressed with our very own treasure of the world's knowledge, even if we could not afford it.

Air Force sergeants don't make much, and as we moved among bases he worked extra jobs to pay for (and keep) the station wagons, school clothes, the used film projector which never worked and encyclopedias... and make partial payments to lawyers in the never—ending custody battle while my father avoided his child support.

In Florida, he cleaned houses, and in Tennessee he worked in a liquor store and washed cars at a dealership. He napped between jobs, 30 minutes of rest before my mother would rouse him for work. Sometimes, he slept in the car while my mother drove him to work. I saw him once asleep in the car in our apartment complex parking lot. I pretended I didn't.

I was a rising junior in high school when we moved to Texas. We were living in a one—bedroom apartment near the Air Force base. It was temporary, my mother said, until a two—bedroom house in a rundown part of town came free in a month. My stepfather got a job cleaning the Dairy Queen.

Sometimes I helped him that summer, but I was a teenager, lazy and resentful, so I avoided going whenever I could find a reason.

We'd get up at midnight, drive a few blocks and park near the road. Afraid I might be seen by someone from my new school, I rushed to the doors to get inside, waiting there in the glare with my back to the road for my stepfather to catch up with the keys.

The lights in the place would be blazing, so I stayed away from the windows in case anyone drove by.

My stepfather scrubbed the grills and appliances and buffed the tile floors until they reflected light like glass. He washed the walls of windows with a rubber squeegee on an extended metal pole. Some nights he would run the ice cream out of the machine and give it to me in a large cup. I can still smell that ice cream these many decades later and won't take my own children to a DQ.

I scrubbed the booths, running my fingers through the creases of the upholstery for loose change. Once I found a dollar bill in the parking lot near our car while I was picking up trash. I also cleaned the bathrooms located behind a swinging metal door in the back of the dining area.

One Saturday night I was filling my soap bucket in the back room when I heard a commotion up front. I turned the water off and heard the metallic clicking and sliding sounds of locks being turned, the heft of the glass door, the sound of air conditioned air whooshing into the night and then, girls' voices, all of them chattering. One of them asked my stepfather if they could use the restroom, which was just a few feet from where I was standing. The girls had to be old enough to drive—my age or a little older. What if they were in my class when I started school in September? They might tell everybody that my stepfather was the janitor at the Dairy Queen.

I heard him murmur and the gaggle of giggling girls grow louder. They were coming. I ducked into the men's room, listening, avoiding seeing myself in the mirror. Through the walls I heard the girls laughing, muffled voices and water flushing. Their door banged open, and their laughing receded like the sound of geese flying away into the distance. I listened to my stepfather relock the front doors, cylinders sliding into place. Through the window in the backroom door I watched headlights sweep the parking lot and veer onto the highway.

"Did you see those cute girls?" my stepfather asked when I emerged.

To him: "I was cleaning the men's room." To myself: "What could you know about cute girls?"

When my mother died I went through her papers to see if

there was anything important to keep. I stacked the photographs I found for my sisters. The old bills, divorce papers, tattered letters to her from when I was in the service and then law school got tossed into the burn box.

I sorted quickly until I found the matchbook, no matches, just the cover, one of those with an advertisement for a correspondence course. For $99, this one promised an "Exciting and Rewarding" career as a "Certified Electronics Technician." I recognized my stepfather's printing, square and childish. He must have kept it in case he ever scraped together an extra $99 for a better life.

I flipped it over between my fingers a couple of times. Knowledge. I was holding it in my hand. I slid it into my shirt pocket just like that dollar bill.

Lost

Cynthia Leslie—Bole

When he said it, Jill was so startled she inhaled her own spit and had to cough it out before she could respond. "What do you mean, lost?" she finally croaked, when her vocal cords worked again. "You've been assuring me this entire day that you know exactly where we are and that the lake is just around the bend!"

Brian looked away and scanned the horizon. "Well, I thought I recognized some of the landmarks, but now I'm just a little disoriented." He hitched up his backpack and tightened the olive—green strap around his waist, as though compressing his middle—aged belly would rectify any navigational inadequacies.

Just as Jill inhaled again to launch into a diatribe, he cut her off. "Now don't go getting all upset, Jillibean. I can definitely figure this one out. Just let me take another look at the topo and I'll make a plan."

"Don't you dare 'Jillibean' me, Brian! All you ever talk about is your glory days as a backpacker, how the wilderness is your home and I must let you show me what you love. You lured me in with your bullshit glowing tales about communing with nature, and now here I am, a city girl with a crashing headache, covered with blisters and mosquito bites, thirsty and out of water, and you tell me we're lost. I put myself in your hands, Brian, like I've stupidly done again and again. Why haven't I learned that your confidence is ill—founded and your suggestions ill—advised?"

Brian flushed and glanced at her, this younger woman he only wanted to impress, this girl he only wanted to take care of and love. "I'll get us outta here, babe. Don't you worry. You just enjoy the view while I chart our course." He unfolded the topo and pulled out his compass, squinting at the glare of the sun reflecting off the map. His eyes were gritty and his tongue thick from thirst. His head was pounding, too.

It had been entirely reasonable to think they only needed one bottle of water each. It was only supposed to be a six—mile round—trip hike to Lake Heron, which had a potable spring flowing into it, and they should have been able to make the hike to the lake in just a couple of hours. He had been so sure. Now he was anything but sure.

Jill snatched the map out of his hands, held her palm out for the compass, and glared at him until he handed it over. "I'm going to take a look at this thing myself," she said. "Can't trust you to navigate your ass out of a paper bag, apparently."

"Baby, you know you can't read maps or use a compass. You've never even been backpacking. Just give them back to me and I'll figure out where we went wrong."

Jill clutched the map to her chest and snarled, "To be brutally honest, Brian, where I went wrong was following you in the first place. First moving to Boston where you assured me I'd find a job, then buying that damn Prius you found that broke down every five miles, then trusting your dear friend Robert friggin' Marshall with my investments, and now going on this damn wilderness fiasco. After nine and a half months, I'm done, Brian."

She stared at the map and noticed the squiggly lines begin to swim. She blinked hard as concentrated tears stung her eyes, then threw the map to the ground.

Jill scowled at Brian, hands on hips, and he dimly noted that her face was red and mottled but devoid of sweat. The phrase "heat stroke" floated through his own boiled brain.

"Sweetie pie, sit down and rest…" he began, but the sound of his voice enraged his girlfriend. Suddenly she spun around and careened away from him in a plume of dust, swinging her arms with exaggerated purpose as she crashed through coyote bush, poison oak and clumps of manzanita.

Brian noticed her hair glinting like polished copper in the sun, not a trace of gray yet, unlike his own, and he felt a pang of longing. But he couldn't follow her. He had never been a follower. He had always been the leader.

He sat down on a boulder and half—heartedly called after her, "Jill, come back. Let's eat some jerky and we'll feel better…" He watched without moving as her magenta sun shirt disappeared into the scrub clotting the chaparral slope.

He just couldn't do it. He just couldn't trail after her, so he sat and stared yet again at the hieroglyphics on the map and tried not to think about water.

The Delivery

Peter Collins

So far, the trip had been smooth and uneventful. A few bumps along the way, but nothing to delay them. It was a pleasant enough August morning, blue skies emerging from a back-ground of long dark clouds, but it was early enough for it still to be cool. Paul was driving. He had seniority and he figured it was his right. He didn't like being a passenger. Not that Bud was a bad driver or anything. Bud was a pro. He wasn't one of these fly-by-night boys they came across now and then. But Paul always felt happier when he was driving. It was just one of those things.

Bud was sprawled out next to him in the front of the cab. He was affecting an air of nonchalance at being in the passenger seat, but in truth he too had wanted to drive that morning. The guys at the depot had ribbed him as they ribbed all the drivers.

'It doesn't matter who's behind the wheel as long as the package is delivered,' they said. Bud knew they were right. Making the delivery on time to the right place was what their business was all about. Nobody cared who drove as long as they got the job done. But the drivers cared. Bud shook his head and tried to focus on the job. It was Monday morning and they had the first package of the week to deliver. Get it done and get on with the week.

They continued for a while in silence, Bud periodically checking the map to make sure they were heading in the right direction. Although the sun was bright, it was still cool in the cab. Bud pulled his jacket around him and shivered.

'This old wreck never gets warm,' he complained.

Paul grinned at him.

'What do you mean "old wreck"?' he asked. 'This is cutting edge American technology.'

Bud grunted. 'Sure,' he replied, 'that's why I'm shivering on an August morning and I have to shout to be heard.' He sank back into his seat in mock despair.

Paul grinned again, but he took Bud's point. It wasn't warm in the cab and despite all the soundproofing, the noise from the engine made conversation difficult.

They must have travelled fifty or sixty miles before Bud spoke again.

'Do you ever think about the job?' he asked simply.

Paul glanced across at him briefly.

'What do you mean?'

Bud hesitated for a moment. 'The job,' he said eventually. 'Delivering things from point A to point B. Not worrying about what we're delivering or why.'

He waved his hand vaguely toward the rear of the vehicle.

'Just making sure this little boy gets dropped off where we're told to drop him.'

Paul looked at his companion. He knew Bud wasn't being literal. There was no child in the back. Bud sometimes had a habit of using coded language and he'd started to refer to the package they were delivering as 'Little Boy'.

'It's our job,' Paul replied simply. He didn't like where this conversation was heading.

But Bud was persistent. 'Doesn't it bother you?' he continued. 'We just make the delivery, but don't you want to know anything about the people who get the packages we deliver? Or how it's going to affect them?'

Paul could see that the idea was bothering Bud. His brow was furrowed and he was struggling to get his words out.

'What I mean is, when we're making a delivery, we could be doing a good thing or a bad thing? Don't you ever think about turning back?'

Paul stared across at him, a touch of concern on his face.

'We're deliverymen, Bud. We can't worry about every package we deliver. We've got our instructions. It's too late to turn back now.'

'But this package is different,' Bud persisted. 'You must know that. Have you thought about it? And if you thought that we shouldn't make this delivery, would you turn back then?'

Paul paused and then nodded his head. He reached out and gently touched his colleague on the arm.

'I have thought about it, Bud. And so have you. We're doing the right thing. You know we are. But when it comes down to it, we're just the delivery drivers. We're going to deliver our package safely and then get home in time for tea. OK?'

Bud stared through the windscreen, as if hypnotised by the clouds ahead of them, and for a moment Paul worried that he hadn't got through. But then Bud smiled and nodded.

'OK Paul,' he said, 'I've got it.'

Paul looked him in the eyes.

'Right, Bud. Then let's get to work.'

Colonel Paul Tibbets sat back in his seat and took the controls of the Boeing B–29 Superfortress named 'Enola Gay' in honour of his mother. Next to him Captain Robert 'Bud' Lewis checked over the radio with the navigator. They were 30 minutes away from their destination, the Japanese city of Hiroshima. Bud nodded to Paul, who gave the order to remove the safety devices attached to the atomic bomb in the bomb bay. 'Little Boy', as the bomb was known, was now armed and ready to be dropped. They flew on towards their target, ready to make their delivery.

Universal Rules

Jenean McBrearty

Even quantum universes have rules. Corky McArdle found out when his yearning for learning led him into a worm hole called The Big Bubble to acquire the esoteric knowledge he'd read about in the Cosmic Times classifieds.

LEARN HOW TO BE A BETTER YOU
Let Guidance Inc give you the answers you seek.
Guaranteed. Not a cult.

As one McGuffin was much like another, Corky caught the shuttle to Know Wonder, the particle that behaves as a wave that can seem as a dream.

"I'm confused," he confessed to the linen–shift, red–robed guru who was asking the standard introductory questions. "Things used to be so simple. Now, I need to know how to be another me at the same time as regular me. Cheery and morose. Shallow and deep. Married and single. I want to be a Schrodinger person. Understand?"

"I understand what you mean," Cloned–Jesus said. "But I usually begin with a name. You are …?"

"If you don't know, I'm in the wrong place."

"I should have been precise. What name did your spawners assign you?"

"Corlander. Corky, for short."

"You can always change it. If you want to continue, step inside the cell analyzer and remove your clothing."

"As in get naked?"

"The analyzer works best that way. It might mistake your sweater buttons for an extra belly button, and add inaccurate information to your card. You don't want an inaccurate card, do you?"

"My birth certificate has wrong information on it, and there's never been repercussions," Corky said as he shrugged.

Guru–Jesus scribbled something in a notebook. "One man's necessity is another's 'I'll get by without it'," he said. "If you're comfortable with a less thorough assessment, we do have a walk–through cell reader."

"Yeah, that's better."

Inquisition–Jesus wrote in his notebook again. "You tolerate inaccuracies but not imprecision. Interesting from a comparative cultures point of view. Can you explain that?"

"Regretfully, I can't explain why anyone would bother with comparing cultures. As for inaccuracies, one can be precise about the distance of the moon from the earth, but be inaccurate — pretend a scientist says it's 238,900 kilometers. It's 238,900 miles or 149,312.5 kilometers. Since it only matters in trivia game shows or travel itineraries, does it matter?" Corky said.

"Perspicacious–ness. That's a trait you'll want to keep."

"Along with a good vocabulary."

"How do you feel about grammar?" Faux–Jesus said.

"I love s'mores made with fresh, crisp grammar crackers."

"And groups?"

"Only for three—s'moresomes," Corky said. "Why so many questions?"

"We tailor our services to match individual needs and preferences. Just one more, I promise. Which three people do you admire?"

Did Synthetic—Jesus mean who were his role models, or who he believed were the greatest people who ever lived? Corky considered asking for clarification. "It depends on what you mean by admire. I admire bathing suit models, but I wouldn't want to be one."

Authoritarian—Jesus tapped his pencil eraser on the desk. "For someone who tolerates inaccuracies regularly, your insistence on definitional split—haired—ness certainly seems petty. Alright, three people you'd like to be like."

"Oscar Wilde because he was witty. George Washington because he was courageous. And Laurence Olivier because he could act."

"I see your problem clearly now. You think of yourself as a half—witted, cowardly ham. That explains your forgiving nature when it comes to cards. What company issued your birth certificate? Let me guess ... Goggle."

"How did you know?"

"We get thousands of their standard AI models. Ordinary men, we call them. They all seem to wind up here desperate to be delivered from their mediocrity. Make me witty, brave and talented, they plead. The names change, but their preferences always boil down to one thing: popularity. The bane of human existence. Lack of it is as powerful as the black plague for creating dread and depression."

"How else can one be popular without being entertaining, funny and overcoming stage—fright?" Corky wondered aloud.

Sympathetic—Jesus cast his dark almond—shaped eyes towards the horizon. "There was a time when people asked for spiritual guidance. Make me kindly like St. Francis. Now, it's make me as wealthy as Gates, handsome as Finn Wolfhard ... very few ask for Solomon's wisdom or Einstein's curiosity."

"I'm curious. Who's Finn Wolfhard?"

"You do have an antiquated card! I see what Goggle did. They used old infobits and put them on a new card in a standard model they peddled as a designer model. I'll bet your spawners paid a hefty price for the rip—off, too. What's the date and place on your birth certificate?"

"Nineteen seventy—two, Berkeley, California."

"And your spawners were Proto—Millennials seeking meaning in their college liberal arts programs." Affable—Jesus smiled. "I'll bet if I check your card, I'll find that one was an English Lit. teacher, and the other taught history at a high school. Am I right?"

"I loved them anyway. What's your point?"

"My point is, Corky, that's probably why you're not popular. Not to put a too Freudian tip on it, you're blah because your parents couldn't teach you how to fit in — because they never fit in. They likely did the best they could with recycled goods they were unaware of, but here you are ... nerdy."

"Can you help me? The ad said guaranteed ..."

Generous—Jesus scanned his notes into his computer, hit a few buttons, and out came a pristine SD card from a slot in a small box to the left of his screen. "I'm going to roll your requests into one, so you'll have two adjustments — we work on genie—time here. No lamp, but you get three wishes, you could say. Take the card through those doors to the back, and the technician will replace your old card with an updated, accurate, and precise new one."

Corky perused his bill. Thirty dollars for the Groucho Marx card. Four hundred for labor. Yes, in every universe he'd traveled, there was a law that read: It's not the parts but labor that makes repairs so expensive.

The Dumps

Zach Murphy

You get stuck driving behind a colossal, sluggish, and stinky garbage truck. You think about all the minor decisions, the split seconds in time, and the winds of fate that came together to lead you to this very moment and place. You poured that extra bowl of Cinnamon Toast Crunch for breakfast. You pooped again right afterwards. You headed out the door to your car and forgot your wallet. You rushed back inside and grabbed it. On the way back out you noticed your left shoe flopping against your heel. You bent down to re—tie the laces. Then your other shoe needed to be tightened too. You bent back down to re—tie your right shoe to balance things out. You slid into your car and that one song you hate was playing on the radio. You scrolled through all the stations and concluded that silence was better than whatever emitted from the airwaves. You drove off and you stopped at that one red light that always takes forever. When the light finally turned green, you pressed the gas and the garbage truck lugged out in front of you. You've been behind it for at least 15 minutes now. It smells like rotten eggs and dirty diapers. Probably because it *is* rotten eggs and dirty diapers. You roll up the windows. It still smells. The garbage truck is plodding 25 miles—per—hour in a 45 miles—per—hour zone. You're running late to the movie screening, even when you consider the twenty minutes of unnecessary previews they show. You can't miss this review assignment, or your editor will fire you. You want to switch lanes. But the traffic is coming on strong. It's risky. Don't try it. It's not worth it. Don't mess up someone else's very moment and place in time. Don't do it. Don't do it. Oh God, you just did it.

Late Awakening

Jan McCarthy

The night before the wedding I find that instead of beauty–
sleeping I'm somehow out of bed and banging my head against
the wall. The pain brings me to my senses.

It's just as well I'm in a hotel room and not with *him*
tonight. He'd have a lot to say, none of which I'd want to hear.
Some traditions to do with weddings have more meaning and
purpose than we realise. The couple in the next room, who I
earlier heard having sex in a way that made me think they were
showing off, wall–knock angrily. They must have thought I
was doing it to annoy them.

This is my subconscious, warning *Not this man*. Not with
this set of rules: be sexy, always elegant, slim, scintillating,
athletic, youthful. *Make me proud to be seen with you. You
should wear this, wear your hair like that. Look at André's
girlfriend. Now, there's a woman who knows how to charm
her man! You should talk to her, get some tips. Apparently she's
a tiger in the bedroom too...*

I move a step to the right, look at myself in the mirror over
the sink. The moonlight silvers me. I'm a ghost, a nobody from
nowhere. But it's like being washed clean. Put away this feeling
of coming disaster. Love conquers all, right? Shift my weight to
the ankle that's strapped up, testing. High heels are the worst in
this Napoleonic city of cobbled streets. I've turned my ankles

more times than I care to count. The bandage'll have to come off for photos. Suppress feelings of terror. Everybody's flying in for the wedding. People have invested. There's a pile of gifts: showy–expensive from his side, quirkily hand–crafted from mine. It's all a bit *Howard's End* to be honest. There's the dress. The flowers. The stretch limo. To go back now would be humiliating. *There she goes again!*

The bruise on my forehead, even under makeup, is visible in the wedding pictures I'm quick to reduce to ashes, at the awakening six months in. He's gone, taking the Christmas savings from the tin on the kitchen table and *my* suitcases. The clock on the wall says half past two, but I can't think where the day has gone. I've done nothing but drink coffee and rid my computer, phone, bookshelves, drawers, cupboards of every–thing of his. The brick–built barbecue, which I'm keeping an eye on through the kitchen window, still smoulders. All his books burnt. Self–help books he placed on the coffee table to lure me.

In case you're a total bastard like Etienne (though I doubt a total bastard would have read this far) here's a tip: the word *hysterical* is useful when you want to make a woman lose her cool.

It was finding the ability to laugh at him that made him leave, in the end. I'd have taught myself the art of amused tittering, loud chortling and gleeful braying weeks ago, if I'd known that was the way to get to him, make him share my rage.

Mandy says I have low self–esteem, and she didn't get that from a self–help book. It's common sense. Big sister Mandy's

out getting in *our* kind of food for the week — the kind of food
I've been denying myself since Etienne swanned into my life
looking immaculate. But who puts knife—sharp creases in their
jeans?

That was one domestic task I *wasn't* allowed: the ironing. I
never did it right, according to him. Another clue was the
washing—up. Three or four times I arrived at his place,
exhausted from the twenty—two hours' travel and found a
mountain of greasy items in his sink, a note pinned above it that
read variations on the same theme: *Gone to see André and
Rita. Make yourself at home.* To my shame, I washed, dried
and put away every single teaspoon, and watched ingratiatingly
for his smile of approval at midnight, when he rolled in, drunk.
I didn't ask him what he'd been doing. He'd have said I was
prying. Once, when I smelt a woman's scent on him and asked
if he'd been cheating, he said I was paranoid, and that if I
carried on like that, it would be *my* fault if he did. I still don't
get the logic of that.

There's pizza on the menu tonight. Ice—cream sundaes for
afters. A bowl of our favourite snacks to go with the trio of
chick flicks we've lined up. We'll put on our matching cow
onesies, slouch on the couch, probably doze off. Tomorrow I'm
getting a new wardrobe: softer fabrics, brighter colours, nothing
clingy. The new me. I'll never be the wimp I was before. They
can call me a bitch, a strident harridan, whatever, but one day
this rage will have ebbed away. Meanwhile I'll find something
productive to put my energy into. Garden'll do for a start.
There's a man coming to take away Etienne's decking, his
trendy fire bowl we never sat by, and the shed where he kept
his porno mags. Mandy and I'll spend happy days creating beds
for bee—loud herbs and rampant roses, a scattering of fruit trees,

an arbour with fat cushions. A meadow strip where wild flowers can run as untamed as they like.

Etienne sent an email from Dubai. He's found someone new. *She* doesn't heehaw like a donkey or use his toothbrush by accident. *She* is *correct. She* is never hysterical. *She* has self–control. I laugh out loud as I read it, and Mandy joins in, between puffs and pants from carrying in all the nosh and booze.

You see, *hysterical* doesn't apply in my case. I'm wombless. A hysterectomy in my late thirties. Don't ask. It happens. So Etienne had to take me seriously when I turned round – finally – and yelled in his face: *Get the holy fucking fuck out of my life!*

Not Quite Ripe

Howard Brown

She was a waitress, he a loquacious hipster who sat at the bar each night drinking gin and tonics, living large off the dope trade in midtown Memphis. It was not exactly love at first sight, but in time a spark was struck and passion bloomed.

She was white, he was black; his mother an English professor at Swarthmore, her dad an over–the–road trucker. Despite the odds against such a match, they hoped that love would conquer whatever obstacles might stand in their way. Still, they were not without some trepidation as they drove from Memphis to her hometown in Mississippi one sweltering Saturday afternoon in July. And when they reached her father's house, she told the boyfriend to wait in the car while she went inside and tested the waters.

She didn't bother to knock, but opened the front door and stuck her head inside. Her father sat in his easy chair, her uncle on the couch, both watching television. "Hey, Dad, Uncle Bunk, what's up?" she asked, tentatively. "Aww nothing, we're just sitting around watching these niggers wrestling on TV," her father replied. "Come on in."

But she didn't. No, she quietly shut the door behind her, walked back to the car and, as she and her boyfriend made their way back to Memphis, it now seemed clear that the time for introductions to her redneck family was not quite ripe.

The Man I Could've Been

J.J. González

I've lived many days, and I knew inside my head that this would be the last I'd see. Could anybody make it to the end without any regrets? Has anybody been so wise and clever they've lived the best life they could have, and if they have, were they happy doing so?

My family surrounded me, or what was left of it. My children, whom I love with all my heart, and their own, were here to see me off. I was so far gone that I couldn't even answer their loving gestures with more than a groan or a whimper, and I could not see them unless they would sit themselves in front of my yellow, milky eyes. Right now, it was my firstborn son, holding my hand, knowing that the end was about to come.

Behind my child, clear as day, I saw another man in the same bed. He looked like me, he was my age, and the same inevitable disease that would eventually make him succumb as well. He was surrounded by his loved ones, though they were many.

With him was the girl from high school I was in love with. He wasn't afraid of asking her out to prom and that was the start of a long, beautiful relationship that had lasted all the way to this point and would probably endure until either of them passed away. She'd aged like wine and given him two healthy boys and a gorgeous daughter, and they all had many children of their own. They all took their turns climbing on the bed to hug their grandfather; they all were genuinely excited to see him. I always wondered what that was like.

At the foot of the bed were his old friends from college. They weren't in the best shape themselves, but they didn't have our curse. The man in the bed knew that he could count on their support whenever he needed it, and that they would be there for his family once he was gone. They sobbed and sighed and hugged each other at the sight of their dear friend deteriorating before their eyes and traded old memories of their fun little escapades from back when they were young, none of which they regretted. I haven't seen them in a decade, at least.

Standing at his right side were his colleagues and interns. He had grown a network since he entered college and worked hard to maintain it by excelling at his job and finding solutions that required thinking outside the box. He was not fond of being on−call all day every day, so he had set boundaries early and was always given his privacy. He'd managed to balance his life and work, and even left the rat race early. The grass was, indeed, greener.

And so, the doctor went to his bed first to tell him the good news. Thanks to his healthy diet and lifestyle, it would be an uphill battle, but he could expect to survive this round. He could even recover in the comfort of his own home. It was unprecedented, of course, but there are always miracles and disasters in a hospital. He got the first and I got the latter.

Everyone around the bed cheered, and they left to give him and his wife some privacy. She kissed him on the cheek, gave him a hug longer than I'd ever had the pleasure to enjoy, squeezed his hand and left the room so he could change and let himself out.

He looked good for his age. Sure, he wasn't sculpted like he was in his youth, but he wasn't a dripping bag of wrinkles and skin like I was. He removed his robe, put his clothes on, looked at the bed, and walked to where I was. Only I could see him, him and all the others who were on the way out of the cold, white hospital room.

"Well, isn't this sad," he said. "Wasting away on your deathbed, just like you wasted all your days on this gorgeous green earth."

"Why am I seeing you? Why now of all days??"

"The greatest punishment before you left was letting the person you became see the person you could've been."

My grip loosened and my family faded out of sight. For a moment, I could only see the best version of myself, staring back at me with pity. He put his hand on my shoulder, understanding of what led me to this situation. Myself.

Finally, I saw nothing.

Wifey Wife

Robert Steward

"What do you mean you have the wrong tickets?" The big, black, middle−aged man at the ticket office jabs his finger at me. "The machine does not make mistakes!"

With his blue suit jacket, peaked cap and downturned lips, he looks more like a military dictator than a British Rail worker. Behind him hangs a *Have you paid?* sign, making him look even sterner.

"Yes, I know." I thank God for the protection of the Perspex glass. "*I* made the mistake."

"So, you want me to change the tickets because of *your* mistake?" His eyes narrow and nostrils flare. "You do realise these tickets are non−refundable."

At this point, I can imagine Maria's shrill voice greeting me on the platform, telling me I never do things properly. Her words sharp like daggers: *"James, non fai mai le cose come si deve!"*

And you know what? She's right. It's the first time her parents have come to visit from Italy in fifteen years, and I can't even arrange a day out to London without messing it up. Not only are the tickets going to cost twice as much, but we're probably also going to miss the train. The day has hardly started and it's already turning into a disaster!

"Well, you see, I'm with my wife and in–laws, and you know what it's like – I got a bit confused and pressed *single* instead of *return* on the ticket machine," I say, looking for empathy.

Just then, his mobile phone lights up and the words: Wifey Wife appear on the display.

Wifey Wife! Can you believe it? *Wifey Wife!*

With smiling lips and dimpled cheeks, his face appears softer, kinder, no longer the short–tempered jobsworth, but a kind, loving husband. He pauses before refusing the call, as if in two minds whether to answer it or not.

"So, you want four returns to London?" he asks in a milder tone, as though nothing has happened.

"If that's possible." I slide the tickets towards him.

He refunds the single tickets and issues me four returns.

Suddenly, there's a cacophony of sound from the loudspeaker, reminding me I don't have much time: "The 10.54 Southeastern service to London Victoria will shortly be arriving on platform four..."

"Is that everything?" he yells through the din.

"Just one more thing. I see the trains are going to Victoria today instead of Charing Cross. Can we change at London Bridge?"

"No, all the trains are direct. You need to take the underground from Victoria to get to Charing Cross."

"The underground?" Beads of sweat roll down my forehead. "But, that means I need Travelcards!"

Hearing this, he gives out a huge sigh, loud enough to shake the ticket office to its foundations, and as we look at each other for what seems like an eternity, I wonder what side of his personality is going to speak next.

Then Wifey Wife calls back.

Staging Post

Eddy Knight

I was down in the bowels of the earth when our eyes first met. I call it that, although it's really the basement level of the museum. The ceiling's low and it's dim in the giant display case where I was working. I'd lowered the lights in an attempt to keep visitors away from this end of the gallery, where I was putting the Cobb and Co coach back together. I don't like being on display myself. So I was annoyed when I looked up and saw, on the other side of the glass, a young Chinese woman looking at me.

My annoyance dissipated instantly when I saw how beautiful she was; her straight black hair pulled back from her smooth and shining forehead, her high cheekbones and her eyes so dark, like ponds at midnight, or starless skies, way beyond depth or comprehension. She must have thought me a mannequin, for she jumped when I looked up, the fine lines of her eyebrows arched. Then her mouth lifted at the corners and she gave a little smile, her lips parted and she silently voiced "Sorry," before moving on.

A simple mistake. Sitting motionless on a log, with a blown-up photo of a desert staging post behind me, I probably looked the part in my flannel shirt and jeans, with sections of the disassembled coach, of an age with the photo, laying on the ground around me. It's the same design as the stagecoaches of

Western movies, rattling their way over distant prairies, to be held up by outlaws or set upon by Indians. It's surprising how small they are when you see the real thing up close, rather than portrayed on celluloid.

Our coach had been displayed for years in a large, north-facing window which looked out onto a side street, and been virtually forgotten there. Constant direct sunlight, and the heat of numerous summers, had caused the paintwork to blister down one side, and the distinctive red and yellow livery to fade. Finally the curator had noticed its sorry state and decided to have it moved.

So it fell to me, as exhibitions technician and all-purpose handyman, to take it apart piece by piece, there being no other way of getting it down the stairs. Now I was sitting inside the giant glass case designed to prevent people from climbing all over it, wishing that I had made more detailed drawings at the disassembly stage. It had seemed so simple and logical at the time: 'you unbolt this piece, and take that bit off, so you can get to the section underneath, which gives you access to that forked contraption behind...' Simple really, like a jigsaw puzzle in reverse. So I hadn't bothered much, beyond taking a couple of photos.

I'd done it deliberately, if I'm honest. I'd wanted the challenge. My life had sunk into a bit of a rut. I enjoyed working in the museum, it was certainly preferable to some of the joinery shops I had worked in, far cleaner for a start, but day-to-day maintenance does get boring. It's only when we're preparing for a new exhibition that the place really comes alive, and that wasn't due for another few months.

My home life was equally uneventful. My wife and I had separated a year before and I hadn't met anyone yet to take her place. I was spending my free time sporadically doing up a ramshackle cottage, which was all that I could afford after the split. It was nothing taxing, mostly painting and decorating, so I had set myself this problem at work, which I was now regretting.

I trust it also explains why I ran after the Chinese girl. To myself at least, for it was totally out of character. I am naturally rather reserved, certainly not given to acting on impulse. It was her smile that did it, that reticent, shy in its own way, gentle lifting at the corners of her lips that elicited such a powerful response. No one had smiled like that at me for a very long time. I tore down the temporary barrier I'd erected to keep the general public out, and followed her down to the far end of the gallery.

Instigating conversations with attractive young women was something that I was way out of practice with, but my apology for startling her seemed to go down well, and led to questions about where she was from, what she did for a living, and all of the usual opening gambits. On learning she was a uni student on holiday, travelling around her family's recently adopted new country to find out more about it, I asked if she fancied joining me for lunch.

My heart leapt when she accepted and we both laughed at that same moment, the pair of us surprised, as I thought, at the suddenness and strength of a mutual attraction. Smiling happily at our new acquaintanceship, we left the museum arm in arm, and made our way up the esplanade until we came to a favourite café of mine, the one with a view out to sea.

Conversation continued to flow easily between us and, although not usually given to drinking at lunch, I ordered us each a glass of wine, to savour while awaiting our order.

Replete, and feeling mellow after plates of fish and chips with salad, the talk became more personal. Overjoyed when she asked if I were married, and not wishing to complicate matters, rather than saying separated I just said, "No."

"That's good," she said, which led me to contemplate taking the rest of the afternoon off.

Any romantic notions were immediately dashed when she mentioned an aunt who still lived in Singapore. Apparently the family was prepared to pay ten thousand dollars to anyone who would marry her, so that she could come over and join them.

I returned to my work, heavy of heart.

John James Carter (Export Manager)

Christine Law

The door was locked. They came, they went. Apparently after the crash, John's brain had stopped functioning normally. Maggie had held his hand for hours telling him about people they knew. No one knew how much he knew. Friends from the Rugby Club had stopped coming. How long had he lain in this comatose state? There was a single bed, with a blue floral duvet and matching curtains. A chair stood by the bed. He must be in a small room; nursing staff came and went. Maggie had told him the walls were pale cream, and the colours of the duvet and curtains. Sometimes the staff woke him up to change the bed, he was like a large baby in pads being fed intra-venously.

Pictures would flash through his mind. He was at primary school, a scholar at Eton, then in the army. There was a scene with him working in an office: what was his job? Scenes where he meets others, entertains them and then he's back in the office. The older couple who come must be his parents? If only his mother would stop crying, her voice sounds like babble. His father tells him all about the staff nursing him: as if he didn't know? They don't know his thoughts and feelings. His eyes fill with tears; his alive Maggie grips his hand. There is hope. The nurse takes his pulse and the doctor arrives.

Maggie will never know how close he came to leaving her that night. His thoughts were a blur. They had been drifting apart as a couple, their life together had become acceptance. Then he had swerved the four-by-four to miss that fox, hitting the verge before the entrance to Matlock Farm. Someone had hit him from behind forcing him to veer into the oncoming traffic. Then everything had shut down. Memories would come and go, but he was alive. They would rebuild their life together. His affair with Suzy the blousy barmaid at the Duck and Hounds would be over.

Patterns from the asylum

Martin Shaw

I turned up for war in my boots, gas mask, and just my underwear on, dancing upon corroded mess tins full of piping hot chicken supreme, my interpretation of an enemy battlefield belching shrapnel and burnt skin. Helicopters spun cloud circles over my head and made a set of spectacles for God to examine his faulty creation. At the same time, abseiling soldiers dropped from thread upon thread upon thread, but only to get stuck in the brown treacle spoils of old blood and guts, like money spiders on a freshly painted windowsill.

You–you–you, hands up, you fucking traitor, one soldier bawled, submachine gun ready and pointing.

I jogged on the spot shouting *Wahey,* and reached for the sky like a preacher, *oh Lordy Lordy.*

Piss taker, another soldier said wiping gut sausage from his shoulder.

No, they weren't German else he would have said, *Hände hoch.*

Free from the mire they all shot me. It fitted in lovely with the surroundings – the leafless black varicose vein–looking trees and dead pigeons scattered like feathered molehills, along with a one–eyed duck blown in half by a daisy–cutter bomb, the other half vapourised into the smell of duck–fat shortbread cookies.

That's not one of the enemy, he must have come the wrong way, I heard someone say as my life ebbed.

Turn back, everyone, cried another. *He's from the asylum because he's wearing paisley underpants.*

Before I kicked the proverbial bucket, I still had time to reply. *Yes, I so hate my y–fronts, don't you? I'm a fan of pinstripe and love the minimal intricacies of its almost invisible lines. They are unobtrusive to one's thoughts, a subtle pleasant–ness even, like an expensive aftershave for the people who get close to you. On top of that, they add mathematical precision to identify each part of my body in case I'm injured, a point of reference for the surgeon, so to speak. Too late now, though, goodbye.*

Asylum or not that was a good call, a soldier commented.

Still alive I managed to reply. *Err, I did say goodbye.*

Immediately they all opened fire again, this time at my groin area.

Last word, dipshit, I heard.

Yes, paisley is terrible, I muttered.

Fire at will!

The Breakthrough

Pam Knapp

No name: not for whom; not from whom. The parcel was quite small but well secured with enough parcel tape to secure the crown jewels.

Whose was it? Pam picked up the small, soft parcel, looked about for the likely patron but found none. Her brow knotted. Ahh, she guessed, it was from Paul. Her husband was a hopeless romantic and letters or cards were often presented for important unoccasions when some mishap with the mortgage or house insurance had gone awry. A mystery offering was a significant raising of the bar, and she wondered what he'd done for her to deserve it. She cagily scanned around to see if he was watching her discovery. Nobody there, but she had heard him pottering in the front garden earlier, for sure. Her heart smiled a little – silly old fool!

Hmmm. It looked to have been made airtight. Perhaps it was perishable. Cake? No, it'd be ruined wrapped around like that – unless it was very small, or biscuity? Grapes? It'd be a very small bunch, if it was. Perhaps three or four figs or a few small kiwis… Ooooh: passion fruit? She gently squeezed the soft parcel hoping to decipher any shapes hidden within it. But no, nothing she could be sure of through the padding. She raised the packet to her ear and shook it a little, listening for muted shifting that would reveal individual, loose bounties. Nothing. No, not fruit then.

Pam weighed the parcel in her palm. Not small or light enough for a silk scarf or boxed up like jewellery. Shame. Perhaps it's that handmade soap she'd raved about at the craft fair, all wrapped around so as not to be guessed straight away. Placing the parcel across the sieve of her fingers, she offered it up, as if her hands ceremoniously held sweet scented water to sweep across her face. Her nose took in a long, deep, deep breath and she held it there for a moment. A whole head full of sensory receptors detected nothing but the sticky residue of tape glue. Another deep inhalation just to be sure, as now soap had become the clear favourite; Paul was romantic but not particularly imaginative. Nothing, not a whiff.

With fingertips at each end of the packet she held it close to her eyes, rotated and inspected it for a gap in the tape that she might use to tear the bag beneath and take a sneaky peek before putting it, centre stage, on the dining room table and pretend that she had thought it had been left for him. She sniggered at their little game – at their age! Who said romance was dead? Frustratingly, there was not one accommodating gap in the tape.

To peel off a little of the tape was her next move and she started to pick away at an edge with a little urgency, lest she be seen and her counter–ruse foiled. The fingers of her left hand wrapped around the small parcel as in strangulation now and those of the right, gouged deep into the supple covering, managing to pick off only miniscule amounts of tape. This would take all day.

Time was pressing now; Paul might appear any moment. She gripped the parcel tightly with two hands, raised the prize to her lips and bared her teeth. She'd bite the wrapping and tape off at one end. Holding the parcel firmly to her mouth like an oversize sandwich, she used her tongue to find a suitable place of purchase for her incisors to shear through. Her lips rolled back, mouth in a wide grimace and nose screwed up to accommodate enough of the parcel end to ensure a firm hold between her teeth.

Paul appeared from the side of the house to remove the packet he'd temporarily left on the doorstep, just in time to see his wife rupture the security of his well−taped plastic bag and watched as the triumphant breach blossomed forth quantities of much−spoiled, thick tissue roll, with which he'd thoroughly cleared a rather large deposit, left somewhat inconsiderately, outside the front of the house by an evidently well−fed dog.

Semi—Colon

Paul Jauregui

A punctuation mark with a value between those of the comma and the full stop and a cause of constant debate between academics regarding its appropriate use.

The writer commits pen to paper and composes a sentence. The full stop will complete it.

The author pauses, and decides that this composition will continue. A semi—colon tells the reader there is more to come. The beauty continues.

This is no longer simply two marks on a page. It has become a metaphor, a symbol of hope and change.

The tortured mind stares into the abyss. A poor soul on the brink of placing a full stop at the end of their own personal sentence.

But if they can summon the courage instead to place on the page of their life that vertical column of two marks and agree to write more, to continue their own beautiful story, then they have taken the first step back from the edge.

And if you can take one step you can take two.

A hundred.

You can live on and make your contribution worthwhile.

Through my own choices and because of friends who've taken that brave backward step — and for those who could not — I carry the semi—colon. A small tattoo that states "I too stood at the edge of oblivion and said 'No' to my personal demons. I carried on and shall continue to do so; adding beauty to the world and helping others do so."

Life is beautiful. We need no premature full stops.

Just a Desert or Just Desserts?

Jacqueline Bartle

Some people live to work, others work to live, but there is a third group, really a subset of the second, who spend most of their lives waiting to live, and for whom real life only exists on the small oases of calm between long periods of hard and frantic work. Walter spent his time hopping desperately between oases, but the intervening stretches of desert were gradually becoming wider and the oases themselves smaller.

Walter didn't lack talent, and his early hopes of success might have come to fruition if he had persevered, but he had too soon become disillusioned and distracted from his aims and now passed long hours toiling miserably in the air conditioned desert of his office just to pay his bills and his debts. He never had any time to linger at oases, or money to spend there. Job satisfaction was something he had heard of but never seen, let alone experienced himself. He thought it must be extinct, like the Dodo.

If anyone had dared to ask Walter's boss, Ruby, about job satisfaction among her employees, she would have replied that if any job was not done to her satisfaction, the individual responsible would soon know it and quickly find themselves unemployed. Unlike Walter, she was not particularly talented, but owed her present position to her cunning and forceful character, and the fear she inspired, which enabled her to bully others into doing her work for her, and then take all the credit herself. She kindly allowed her staff unlimited hours of unpaid overtime, and never bothered with unimportant details, such as job descriptions, that might cramp her style.

For some reason, the turnover of employees in Ruby's department was very high. Walter was now the longest serving, because he was too cowardly to leave. He feared he would never get another job due to his (relatively) advanced age and the bad reference Ruby automatically gave everyone who left. For someone so efficient at both his and Ruby's work, Walter was sometimes frustratingly dim, and had not yet realised that all the local employers knew Ruby by reputation, and never even read, much less believed, any reference she gave.

So Walter kept his job by obeying Ruby's every command and she, realising what a treasure she had found, had gradually come to rely on him. She now automatically forwarded all her emails to him, and was rarely seen in the office. Thanks to Walter, her life had become one long happy stay at a five-star oasis, with no intervening trips to the desert. She took long sunshine holidays and often gave orders to Walter sitting beside a swimming pool, cooling drink beside her, while he toiled away in the parched desert she had created.

But even Walter had his limits. The final straw came, when, just as he had finished unravelling a particularly difficult piece of work, which had taken all day, and should have been dealt with by someone much more senior, Ruby called with two new commands. He was hot, tired and thirsty, but instead of going straight home for a few hours of relaxation, and a cold beer, he had to make two lengthy detours, first to collect

Ruby's suit from the dry cleaners, and then her daughters from drama class.

He had had enough, applied for a vacancy in another company a friend had told him about, and soon heard that he had got the job. As soon as he told them where he worked, his interviewers expressed sympathy, and did not mention references. He would soon be able to enjoy the things other people called "weekends" and "a social life".

Walter wrote Ruby a carefully worded email of resignation. At least, it started off carefully worded, but somehow the words "lazy", and "exploitative" and the phrase "You're too idle even to read your emails" crept in. He pressed "send" and strode defiantly out of the office. Then his phone stopped working. Normally he would have panicked, but today it made him happy, as it would now be much harder for Ruby to reach him.

But, his joy was short−lived. Waiting for him at home was a letter from the new company saying that, due to staff cuts, the job he had applied for no longer existed, the employment offer was cancelled, and apologising for any inconvenience caused.

Walter now faced the inconvenience of being unemployed. In sheer terror, he thought of all his debts and bills, unpaid. He saw himself out on the streets, homeless. Why had he ever applied for that job? Weekends and social lives were vastly overrated. If only he hadn't written that email.

But perhaps it wasn't too late. Maybe Ruby hadn't seen his email, and he could somehow recall it. Trembling he opened his laptop, and switched it on. But to his horror it wouldn't work. He tried everything he knew including switching it on and off again, but he couldn't access his emails. And his phone was still dead.

Cursing all technology, he rushed to his office in a panic. The security guards grinned sympathetically as they let him in. They knew Ruby and were used to seeing him at all hours. He began frantically to scroll through his emails. To his horror, he saw that Ruby had already replied. He had to open her message, even though he dreaded what she had to say.

But what he read quickly turned his fear first to explosive fury, and then to confusion. It seemed to prove that Ruby really was lazy, and didn't read her emails. Or was it her way of refusing to accept his resignation? For the message was the same one he always saw on everything Ruby sent him. Short and to the point, it said,

"Walter, please action this."

The trouble was, this time he wasn't sure how to.

Highway Dogs and their Owners

Erica Plouffe Lazure

Too many dogs' heads hang out of car windows today. "They're gonna die, Mama," Charlie says. He presses his hand on the windshield, as if to ward away their future pain. "Canine decapitation!" he says, repeating the phrase he'd learned last month from the newspaper.

But the dogs we see don't die today. Instead, their tongues hang from their wide smiling jaws, catching errant bugs at sixty miles an hour, fur blowing crazy–cat, no seatbelt. Charlie can't stop watching them, their easy freedom, their faun–spotted sleekness, their curly mop tops. One satin black lab, thick skin pink tongue, wears a silver chain choker that tamps his rest stop curiosity. "What are the owners thinking?" Charlie says, as the lab bounds untethered from his car window, nose first, followed by a young man, off to the poop park.

"Maybe the highway is too much today," I say. Charlie nods, and I check the GPS, and find a way to Camp Tuckaway off the main highway. In ten minutes we are on the back road along the Poconos, "avoiding traffic," Charlie says, looking out the window at the lush hillside, the green luster of summer. He should be excited for camp, but I know he is instead thinking of the highway dogs and their owners, so delighted and free and together they don't think a thing about an open window on a sunny day. *Collie in the front seat*, I hear him think. *Dog is My Co-Pilot*—playing out the possibilities of his dad's last few moments in the car with Collie. *Car accident on I-95. Oncoming vehicle. No survivors.* He'd spent an hour reading that newspaper article, looking up each word, building the vocabulary for his grief. It's when we spot a fawn trailing his mama across the road in a canopy of trees, that Charlie heaves out a sob. I pull over, folding his body into mine, as the fawn glances in our direction, curious, before he's nosed by his mother to press on.

Second Chance

Lois Perch Villemaire

I take my place at the end of line behind the sign "Second Chances". Word has spread of today's special event and the announcement states that interested souls must arrive before noon. I glance at my wrist monitor to confirm that I have ten minutes to spare. I expected the line to be long but couldn't get here any earlier. Today is a workday. Because of my back−ground, I've been assigned to work in the Grand Records Repository, the location for documentation. It's all there for me to research and maintain, both the past and future.

Noticing golden eagles looming in circles on high and angels adorned with their finest wings serving as crowd control on the ground, I mulled over my request. Rules are to state the request in 100 words or less, to be mind−read for the master administrator.

I have been in the Everlasting for 15 cycles. Being here is comfortable. I'm not looking to go back. I miss everyone but in time they will join me. My transition to the Everlasting is cloudy to me. In my final moments, I recall crossing a street on a shopping trip, then a massive jolt and darkness fell, like a heavy theater curtain. I was probably hit by a vehicle.

I'm requesting a loftier reason for being swept away, a second chance to do better. I wish to save the life of another by my demise, and most importantly, I wish that the individual go forward to do phenomenal things for the betterment of the aggregation of inter−planetary society.

My records indicate there is a boy capable of such greatness due to his curiosity, photographic memory, keen mind, and attitude of kindness. He finds learning easy and flies through requirements with extraordinary accuracy and speed. He is drawn to the study of biology and the workings of the human and non−human body. His life holds so much promise. I have foreseen he has the skills and dedication to finally perfect a cure for cancer − the dreaded cell multiplication and mutation disease that strikes many random souls. The old and young arrive in the Everlasting after fighting and losing an exhausting, agonizing battle with this demon.

The boy needs to stay in existence but flashing dark signals reveal that his bright light is in danger. I hope to be granted a chance to protect him so he can accomplish the essential work he is meant to complete.

My turn comes to face the master administrator. He places each of his index fingers on my temples and we both close our eyes. My mind and heart unfold and I sense his reactions of positivity and acceptance.

The cheering of the fans becomes a collective roar awakening my attention. I'm at a major league baseball game. I stand up for a better look at my surroundings. My seat is just behind the home team dugout on the third base side. Over the noise of the crowd, I hear the crack of the bat and out of the corner of my eye, I see the boy seated to my immediate left. A wicked line drive foul ball rockets into the stands. My head is situated directly between him and the path of the ball. The impact fractures my skull and tears a blood vessel in my brain. It's quick and again the curtain falls.

The boy leaves the stadium covered with my blood splatter. He is unscathed and alert after witnessing such a tragic accident. Imagining himself on duty in an emergency room, I know he is even more certain about following his dreams to a future in medicine.

Protection

Ahmed M. Al–Asa'adi
translated by Essam M. Al–Jassim

My parents split up when I was seven. I remember it vividly. I endured a life divided between two homes after my mother remarried.

I then became the object of the family's disputes and the source of ongoing conflict between my father, mother, and cousins.

Each party laid claim to me as their responsibility. Gone was all hope of a normal childhood, filled with unconditional love. Instead, I became a puppet for everyone to fight over, to occasionally play with.

Meanwhile, a monster grew inside me, and no one noticed.

The beast within revealed itself through bouts of extreme violence.

I began to find a strange pleasure in torturing those closest to me. It's as if I'm avenging something I cannot name.

Last night, I killed my father.

I don't know why I did it. Maybe simply because it was he who committed the folly of bringing me into existence. I had to punish him for doing that. Now do you know the importance of using a condom?

It's late. I have to finish what I've started. There are still others who will join my father in hell tonight.

I wonder if the imam who officiated at my parents' wedding ceremony is still alive?

Caught In It

Louella Lester

I have every confidence in you. You can do it. So don't worry your little head at all, a girl can do this just as well as a man, if properly trained—by a man—haha. And even if you screw up, and break the machine, it doesn't matter because this machine is a piece of shit and whatever the insurance company payout is, is likely more than it's worth. Plus, the boss likes you, I've seen him watching you when you walk away, haha. But, you don't want you getting injured, that's for sure. Now, before you push that silvery button to turn things on, haha, turn things on, haha, you have a few safety checks to make, like checking that your sleeves are rolled back and there's nothing that can get caught in the rollers. You never want to gloss over safety checks. See this scar on my thumb? I didn't sleep much one night, not because of anything exciting, haha, but because it was a full moon and I never sleep well when there's a full moon, and I wasn't noticing things and, boom, my sleeve got caught in the rollers. Lucky for me, I accidentally bumped into the button as I was being pulled over the top and it shut everything off before I got sucked all the way in there. Okay, your sleeves look perfect, that's a girl. Then check that the rollers are cleared of debris. Debris means the bits of wood or plastic left in the rollers after the last batch went through. They could end up flying loose and hitting you or someone else, like me, and that wouldn't be good, honey. Alright, looks good, just like you, haha, now before you start it up, and you can't hear me anymore, you have to—hey—HEY!

DIP YOUR GLASSES IN SOAPY WATER TO PREVENT THEM FROM MISTING WHEN YOU DON YOUR SURGICAL QUALITY FACE MASK

Alex Reece Abbott

So you can read more handy hints, like the laminated WASH YOUR HANDS posters and the decals on the garden centre linoleum that remind you how TWO METRES is actually much further apart than you thought. Be couth, dip your glasses, so you can clock that WRONG WAY sign on the door that made them turn you back today. And because there's already too much you cannot see, like the SOURCE DATA behind the colourful, wiggly graphs on the television and the creep of the R NUMBER across your county and THE virus with his suckers out catching a ride on a DROPLET − ready to dock and colonise you. You want to spot the spread of

MASKNE blooming on your cheeks. And you want to see so you can stay ALERT, because without even realising that you are doing it, these days you scan your social contacts, divide your PODS into compliant/non-compliant and symptomatic/asymptomatic and negative/POSITIVE and DIP YOUR GLASSES.

Hair Loss

Jodi Pilcher Gordon

I was ok in myself, until then.

Suddenly, with one horrified reaction I was far from ok. As for my self, it was changed.

It was the way she reacted. The disgust she felt was unequivocal, I'd call it unbelievable, but it was also undeniable.

Disgusted. (noun)
Definition: Inbuilt reaction to something tasting shameful. Can be divined by the reactive curling of upper lip.

The sight of my bald head was so repulsive to her that she couldn't actually allow it, it left a dire taste in her mouth.

In many ways I'd forgotten that no one else saw it, although that was of course the plan. No one knew that under this finely combed arrangement was an aged pate, smoothly barren as an egg.

She flew her hand up to her mouth as if to ward off the shameful sight, then it covered her eyes: 'Put it away!"

Put away your shame, cover your disgusting self, how distasteful of you to get old......

I suppose if I'm old then so is she, but, no, I think if I'm old I'm no longer the 'me' she needs me to be.

How can I be that young boy, the one with all the potential, with his life so very much ahead of him, if I'm actually a middle–aged man? Suddenly my choices seem unwise, my actions inappropriate, my dress–sense plain odd.

Suddenly I'm creepy, I'm a grotesque figure, a playboy sybarite without the means.

I'm officially a Peter Pan, and a dandy of epic proportions. Now I'm hiding something, I'm pretending, I'm a cuckoo in the youth club nest.

In the aftermath I ponder the fact that I've been hiding for so many years now, I can't truly remember when it started.

What's changed is now, in being seen, now I'm one of the guys with a toupée and a fear of the wind.

Now, I'm my age.

And we've never acted it.

At the clothing row

Nneoma Ike—Njoku

At the clothing row, I stopped at a shop with many shirts displayed on hangers in front. The owner of the shop was a bald man in a European—style shirt that fit so closely I could see the folds around his stomach. His smile cracked his face open when he saw me, and he leaped from in front of a sewing machine to welcome me.

"We have it," he cried, extending his hands energetically towards me. "Any style you think of, and if you no find it here, we sew it."

I looked around the stacks of clothes that lined every inch of the wall inside the shop. "I'm looking for a formal shirt," I said. "For my work."

"Ah, a working madam? I said come inside, we have it." He led me to a low stool leaning near the door and I sat down.

The inside of the shop was lit by a single, naked bulb, and a small standing fan produced a low droning noise. At my entrance, a girl and a boy scurried up from where they had been perched near a door the bald man now disappeared into. They were clutching pieces of cloth they looked to have been sewing. The girl followed the man through the door, while the boy remained with me. The bald man soon emerged, holding in one hand a glass of water, though I hadn't asked, and a stack

151

of brightly colored shirts. The girl followed him with another stack of shirts.

I thanked him for the glass of water and, without drinking, set it beside the stool. The man set the first shirt against his stomach and watched my face.

"This one is French design," he said. "Very fashionable." The shirt was a bright orange I thought looked like the inside of a ripe melon. I shook my head, no. The next shirt was a simple one in contrast. It had a layered collar and buttons of the same material as the shirt. I agreed to try this one on, surprised when in the cracked mirror at the back of the stall the shirt did not make me look like a tiger moth. When I returned to the man and asked the price of the shirt, he laughed and waved his hands dismissively.

"It's nothing, my friend. You don't want to try the rest?" He pushed another shirt towards me.

I shook my head. "I have to go home."

"I understand, Madam. We all have to work to eat. It's just three."

"Three what?" I asked. Perhaps my shock showed on my face. The bald man laughed. "This is the new style," he said. "Butterfly shoulder. If you no buy, somebody will buy it faster." He was already reaching for the shirt. I thought I liked the shirt. I could come back here after work tomorrow and buy it. But what if he was right, and someone else bought it? The bald man took the shirt from my hand and put it on its hanger.

As if reading my mind, he said, "Come tomorrow and it would have disappeared. You will not find any shirt like this anywhere."

I took a deep breath and counted out the money, before handing it over to him. He cut off the shirt's tag with his teeth and put it in a nylon bag one of the children brought. As I headed through the clothing row, I saw the same shirt on the door of a stall I walked past. It was a purple one; I thought at first perhaps the blue was harder to find. But by the time I got to the end of the market and to the bus stop, I counted five blue shirts exactly like the one the bald man had sold me. I did not stop to ask how much they were because I was already running late getting home, and it makes no sense to break your own heart.

U–Haul Going Nowhere

Steve Carr

Having sold most of his belongings while sitting at a card table set up in front of my apartment building, all Eric had to do was pack what remaining possessions he had into the back of the smallest U–Haul truck that they rented out and that he could afford. Even with not many things left in his apartment, getting the assortment of clothes, books, framed photographs and his television and computer from the sixth floor of the building down to the truck took him half a day. The building didn't have an elevator so every item had to be carried in his arms down the winding staircase. Because he had OCD, he counted each step going down, and each step as he went back up.

"Don't worry, you'll make it," his downstairs neighbor, Mrs. Slotmeyer, said as he passed her. She stood in her open doorway watching him breathlessly huff and puff as she cheered him on, going up and coming down.

Eric's friend Ted stayed on the sidewalk drinking beers and making sure none of his things were stolen from the back of the open truck. "You're getting there, buddy," he would say with a supportive pat to Eric's back as he added each new armful onto the obsessively, neatly packed possessions he had already managed somehow to cram in. He had planned to leave town by noon, but Mrs. Slotmeyer wanted him to have a piece of fruitcake with her before he left. Since it was leftover from

Christmas she had just taken it out of the freezer and had to let it defrost before they could actually bite into it.

By nightfall Eric was ready to go.

"Where ya headed?" Jack Mackey, the equally OCD runner who jogged exactly the same distance up and down the street the exact same time every night asked while running in place with his head stuck in the passenger side of the truck cab.

"Tucson," Eric said while gripping on to the steering wheel, trying to sound more optimistic then he felt. Even though he had the route and every stop along the way perfectly planned on the map, he had never been to Tucson. In fact, he had never even been to the state of Arizona. His hand seemed incapable of turning the key to get the truck started.

"Why you going there?" Jack asked, still bouncing up and down like a deranged rabbit.

"Everyone has to spread their wings and fly at some point in their lives," Eric said.

"I guess so. Good luck to you," he said, leaving the window and continuing on his run.

"Thanks," Eric said.

He could spread his wings any time he thought, as he got out of the van, unpacked his things, and carried them back up to the empty apartment.

My Stepsister's Porno

Jonathan Slusher

The guy under the Pabst Blue Ribbon neon in a distressed t−
shirt with a cat taco image came pretty close to hitting the
mark.

"The difference is that Betty Schneider cut off his balls," he
said. "The other woman cut off the dude's—whatever his name
was—his junk."

"John. Wayne. Babbit," I spat it out. Ten years plus and
that stupid name was still a punch in the guts. Everyone is
connected to someone famous somehow.

The twenty−something old man with an emoji police line
up hoodie nodded like John Wayne Babbit had been right there
on the tip of his tongue all along.

Waxed mustache choked down a contemplative sample of
sour beer. He'd sent the last one back because it wasn't
carbonated enough. "*Babbit?*" he asked.

"Yeah, like *rabbit*," I said.

The touched by fire waitress had only one table to serve.
Her cut up denim cutoffs exposed pink undies at a coverage
level I'd estimated at about eighty percent.

It was crazy. I was the only one paying any attention.

It was an alien world. Passion had bled out. Voter turnout
of the under−thirty crowd remained far below the threshold to
make it even laughable. A whole generation needed a

precordial thump. Hipsters had flatlined. Something needed to be done fast. I pulled the pin and sat on my own grenade. *Get a load of this.*

"My stepsister was in a porno with John Wayne Babbit," I announced.

"With John Wayne Babbit?"

"They sewed his dick back on. And she *used to be* my stepsister," I set the record straight. "My stepmom divorced my dad so, this is really my ex—stepsister we're talking about."

A true—life low—income vintage 1980s story grabbed their attention enough to keep them all from zoning out back into their screens. That was a pleasant surprise.

Damage report: some millennial attention spans still functional.

I dared anyone to suggest that it was *really* my mom that was in the porno. That was a defensive habit, an over—heightened fear of personal attack was unnecessary these days. Bar room insult leading to physical violence had faded away along with the haze of second hand smoke.

Cat Taco provided a generalized back story of the girlfriend cutting off John Wayne's number. He had been abusive or something. She threw his junk from a moving car into the bushes. Cops found it. It got sewed back on. Then he had been in a porno movie.

"But he wasn't in just one porno. My stepsister starred in *John Wayne Babbit Uncut.* That was his third film."

"Did you watch it?" Waxed Mustache wanted to know.

Awkward silence ensued. When you looked beyond his handlebars Waxed Mustache had pinched eyes that resembled Mike Pence.

I simply nodded an affirmative. Maybe I was trying too hard, but neither the question nor the VP were worthy of verbal responses. *John Wayne Babbit Uncut*, of course I'd watched it. Pushing play on the VCR had been one of the greatest regrets of my life.

From ages nine to seventeen my stepsister and I had leaned dangerously close towards each other's birthday candles. I had stumbled along feeling for a way out. But she had danced weightlessly across the trailer trash surface of our childhood. She turned vending machines at auto repair shops and hospital waiting rooms into bank vaults with secret code panels.

Punch in two more sevens and get ready for the score of our lives!

She knew the broken rules of the game that our parents were playing.

We can't give Grandpa a ride home because he has crabs again…

I was ashamed of what I felt for her. She could have torn my pre–teen heart to shreds at any moment but never did.

"Believe it or not, socially intelligent porn star is not an oxymoron," I informed the group.

They could take that informational nugget and deposit it into their online gaming loot bins.

After the DVD came out I had known the image of my stepsister's head bobbing up and down on John Wayne Babbit's lap would haunt me forever. That knowledge couldn't stop me from watching it. JWB's punchable face relaxed into the seventh state of nirvana was the rotten cherry that sat for years atop my teetering refuse pile of regret.

"If any of you asks me if my stepsister is hot…"

The story of my life, they laughed as if it was a joke.

And maybe it was. I was the outsider. I was the one who didn't fit in. I was the one who couldn't stop hitting rewind and flipping the coin. There was stinging shame on one side and gritty pride in surviving mostly intact on the other.

Then I laughed along too. The best jokes were usually at least partial truths. I was older than them, but I wasn't old. And my serotonin uptake was now inhibited in a way that seemed to be smoothing out the rough times. That was something to drink to. I was a married guy with two kids with a couple of hours to spare. These days I could feel fine after just two.

The sputtering conversation settled into a comfort zone of its very own.

Isn't it weird that all porn actors are called stars?

No, I haven't talked to her in years, but we're friends on Facebook.

Actually, she's doing well. I'm really proud of her.

I don't know if she knows that.

I guess I could send her a message.

I placed a hand on my chest and swore that I would.

Restart Again

Barbara Schilling Hurwitz

I knew it was over when my car skidded into the lake. I should never have had that first drink, but that payday cash itched in my pocket. Teased, taunted, dared me. I didn't want to do it. Well, maybe I did. But I definitely should have accepted that ride home from the bar.

I pushed the door against the water fighting to keep me captive, squeezed my way out and swam a few short strokes to shore where I plopped myself on the soggy embankment and lay back thinking, now I could use a drink.

I was fourteen when I started filling my parents' vodka bottles with water. As the years passed, I moved on to weed and pilfering cash from my mother's purse. The weed grew to coke, and the coke to crack, but I never gave up on the vodka or stealing from Mom's purse.

I hated being a disappointment to my parents, and convinced them if I could just get clean, I would make them proud. That was the first time they shelled out thousands to purge me of my demons.

Cleaned up, I got a job singing and playing my guitar in a local pub. Though frowned upon by my therapist, I was sure the alcohol would not disturb me. For the first few weeks, I showed up early every night and sang my heart out. I was a success. People loved me, and I was even developing a following. Mom and Dad came to see me perform. They smiled and applauded with the audience. They were proud.

It wasn't long before the smell of the whiskey and weed became irresistible, and my meager income way shy of what I needed for my fledgling crack addiction.

After Mom's diamond ring went missing, and the police searched the house for evidence of a burglar, I heard my parents arguing. Dad was convinced I had taken the ring and sold it for drugs. Mom defended me. And having lost all sense of respon−sibility for my actions, I raced to my room to make sure my guitars hadn't been stolen.

Dad was soon shelling out more money for rehab. This time I was committed to leaving that ugly past behind, deter−mined to make something of myself as I had promised.

Once again, I was singing at the club, the only job I could find. There I met Rhonda, and she clung to me like hot glue. She recognized my talent and spoke of my future success. We drank iced teas, and she talked about her life mission to find talent, to protect the abused and to lead the astray on the path to redemption, to success.

I can't remember a fucking thing about how it all came about, but one day we were standing barefoot on the sandy beach reciting vows under the bright white light of the sun, the Caribbean Sea lapping at the shoreline behind us. The heat was intense, my white linen shirt was soaked with sweat, and I couldn't wait for the preacher to declare us joined in holy matrimony. I almost forgot to kiss the bride before I turned and ran into the sea. The thought of never returning crossed my mind, but somehow, I was back on shore in dry clothes spiking my iced teas with vodka.

Rhonda tried to help me, but my resistance grew and arguments became physical. She insisted she couldn't do it alone. She wanted my parents' help. So in lieu of another rehab, we moved to New Orleans where my Mom and Dad put a down payment on a "fixer–upper" house for us.

The work was supposed to keep me busy and out of trouble along with caring for our three dogs and attending daily AA meetings. It worked for a while, but the marriage was crumbling and Rhonda was soon finding comfort in the arms of another man. That's when I never wanted her more. I wanted the dogs, I wanted the house, and I was willing to fight for it all.

And that's what I was thinking when the flashing red lights drew near. "What happened, here, boy?" a deep voice said.

Boy? I thought. "Well, I was rounding this curve, I guess a bit too fast, and my car skidded off the road." My speech must have been slurred because the next thing I knew, I was exhaling into a breathalyzer.

"How much you had to drink tonight, son?"

"Only one, maybe two drinks, that's all. I mean I was definitely sober enough to drive."

"Yeah, well that's not what this test indicates. Ya got a license on ya?"

I grimaced peeling my expired license from my wet shirt pocket, rambling in my defense that it had been reinstated. "I just grabbed the wrong one when I left for work this morning."

"Umhm," the cop said.

I must have asked them to call Rhonda, because as EMTs were stowing me into the cargo bin of their vehicle, I could hear the cop saying, "She's his wife." Then the doors of the ambulance slammed shut.

My head was spinning. I couldn't shut out the noise around me, bright lights shining in my eyes, scissors cutting through my wet clothes, when a warm hand wrapped around mine.

"Rhondie," I whispered, fighting back tears. "Thanks for coming. I'm so sorry." And then like a baby I sobbed in my mother's arms as she broke the sad news. "She's not coming, son. It's over."

Three days later Mom entered the detox ward. I laughed nervously and began singing, "Ho−omward bound, I wish I were…"

"But homeward bound you ain't," she interrupted, shaking her head.

"I'm gonna make it this time, Mom. You'll see."

She was wearing a Tough Love t−shirt, just like the man behind her who stepped forward saying, "Yes, son, this time you will."

Disorientation

Mantz Yorke

A glorious August morning on the northwest of Skye, just right for an after–breakfast meander across the rough heather from the holiday let to the cliff overlooking Oisgill Bay. About the mid–point of the mile or so the map suggested, a golden eagle rose from the heather, probably disturbed by my approach. I caught a glimpse of white patches on its wings, indicating that it was a juvenile, before it became black against the blue sky. I marvelled at its effortless gliding, circling ever higher on the updraft from the cliff ahead. I stood and watched until it drifted out of sight, then resumed my walk to the cliff edge some six hundred feet above the tumble of rocks fringing the sea. Peering down at the black rocks and the lacing of the waves as they burst against them, I didn't notice the fog coming in, until the rocks and sea suddenly became invisible. With the sun and sky now also obscured, I took the hint that it was time to make my way back to the house. A straightforward matter, I thought: though I hadn't taken a compass with me, all I needed to do was to keep the slight sea–breeze at my back and I'd be bound to reach it. I tramped through the heather for some time, becoming increasingly uneasy that I had not yet reached the road that ran parallel to the cliffs. Eventually I broke out of the fog, only to find myself some distance along the hypotenuse of a triangle instead of making the direct return at right angles to the road on which the house stood.

I'd read about aircraft pilots trying to find their way in poor visibility and mountaineers finding landmarks suddenly blotted out, and knew that disorientation can rapidly occur in such circumstances – sometimes with disastrous results. Here, there was no real danger: however, the direct experience of the fog made me appreciate, much more sharply than the accounts in books had done, the need to be able to navigate yourself to safety when you find yourself deprived of the guidance that landmarks provide. I now keep a compass in my rucksack, just in case the elements turn a ramble into something much more challenging.

Daily List

Joan Leotta

Let's see now, my friend Jillian says I will accomplish nothing if
I do not make a list. So I did,
    and now the list comforts me.
    Pack my underwear. One set per day for a one—week stay.
    Pack two skirts
    Pack three blouses
    Pack one pair of slacks
    Pack one sweater
    Pack two pair of shoes
    Some cash
    A journal
    A pen for the journal
    The suitcase is out back, under a bush in the garden.

My second list (in my pocket not the suitcase)
    I'm repeating over and over to myself what Jillian has told
me to do. I put the suitcase list, along with an extra pen, and
money I've saved in my left—hand pocket so George will not
see it.

I look at the list George has prepared for me this morning. It's just for groceries. He will have my chore list ready later today, I'm sure.

Eggs

Bread

Milk

Maxwell House, (His favorite brand of coffee)

Corona, (His favorite brand of beer, one six–pack.)

I put this list in my right–hand pocket along with the twenty–dollar bill George has left on the table. (He *will* count the change, matching it against the receipt, when I get home.)

George is already ready to go. He calls out, "Hurry up!" We get into the car and drive to the grocery.

He asks to see the list and the money. I take them out. After he reviews them, he flips the auto–lock to "open" so I can get out.

"I'll wait in the parking lot," he says, "Don't take too long. It's Saturday and I have games to watch."

I nod.

The other piece of paper weighs heavily in my left pocket as I walk into the store. I know he is watching. Does the paper and pen make a bulge in the coat?

Once inside, instead of heading to the egg case, I meet Jillian by produce. She smiles at the produce manager. We slip through the "employees only" doors to the back of the store and exit from the loading dock where her car awaits.

As we drive off, I lower the window and begin to relax in the cool fresh air. Jillian reminds me, "Jorge will bring your suitcase later today. He dresses as a gardener, so neighbors will take no notice of him. He's probably picking up your suitcase right now. He's the only man we allow to have the address."

I smile and thank her. I have escaped. I am free now. I relax, knowing this change was right.

We continue in companionable silence. When we arrive, she honks the horn twice, speaks into a microphone at the gate. It swings open almost instantly. Before she motors through, up the drive, Jillian reaches into her purse, pulls out a piece of pale green paper, and hands it to me.

"I think you'll like living here at 'The Sister Servants of the Better World'. This is our daily schedule and the list of what we require of all of our neophytes."

Finding Home

Diana Allgair

On our first month anniversary, he broke up with me because I told him my feet hurt after a night of dancing in heels. We resolved things, and everything seemed fine. He started a monthly tradition after that of ending our relationship every time we disagreed. An empty apology renewed our faith in one another, only to have it shattered in another thirty days. Excuses pile high when emotion clouds judgment, and my denial led to my demise.

My family adored him at first. Then they learned the truth of his actions. My friends told me, "You deserve better." Even he said the same on more than one occasion.

Then he kicked me out of our place.

Weeks prior, we planned a trip for my family to meet his family for the first time. That, of course, was canceled. I pleaded with his mother to let me stay for one more week until my family came out. She told me this was for the best and that I needed to be out by that Monday. I had three days to pack everything I owned into my car. My stepfather flew out to drive me, and we made our way across the country back home.

The man I once loved called me the next day. He asked, "Would you have come back if I chased you?"

I answered, "No."

After a few months of promises of change, we tried again. I believed in love over all the warnings, even over my wounded pride. He spoke of marriage and intended to propose to me. Then he broke up with me that same day. Even after that, I tried time and time again. I thought a relationship should last through all things. I didn't understand that this man's inability to love himself meant that he would never love me.

We ended things three years and six months into the relationship. This man pushed me away, but I always came back. This time I did not, and I will not. I pushed the reset button to break this endless loop of heartache.

Regret is not the word I would use to describe the outcome of our relationship. I learned so much about myself and how loyal I can be, if not to a fault. I built such high expectations of where I needed to be in life at a certain age that I didn't stop to consider that the man I fell in love with was not the person for me. I traveled down the wrong path three years ago, and I started my way back. I am the only one who can change the path I walk, and I forgot that.

After waves of heartbreak, I finally stood up and remembered.

The Smell of Ketchup

David Cook

The man next to Debbie smells of ketchup. The odour of tomatoes wiggles up her nostrils as he sleeps, head back, tongue lolling, 50,000 feet above – she checks the little screen in front tracking the plane's progress – Austria, apparently. She wriggles her nose. The aroma is getting on her nerves. She's never been that keen on ketchup. Everyone thinks she's weird when she says that. Her friend Fi's always saying, 'How can you not like ketchup?' Like Debbie's some sort of alien.

Overhead, the little seatbelt light flashes on. Debbie sighs and fastens herself in. The plane thrums up and down and a steward checks everyone is buckled up. He casts a look at Debbie's neighbour, establishes he's strapped up safely, then wrinkles his nose and looks at her sympathetically. She shrugs.

Maybe she should watch a film. She doesn't really like these little monitors, though. She can never get them at quite the right angle and then, if she does, the person in front always shoves their seat back so she ends up having to squelch down and crick her neck while she watches.

The man is still sleeping, snoring softly. A dollop of drool is slowly rolling down his chin. She watches it, wondering how long it will take for it to fall from his jawline and drip onto his blue shirt. The smell of ketchup is stronger.

The seatbelt light has flicked off once again, so she unbuckles. Holy hell, these seats are uncomfortable. She can't wait for this flight to be over. Except, also, she hopes it never ends.

She takes her book from her bag and opens it. She's quite a way into this one. She reads the page, realises she can't remember anything that just happened, then reads it again. No, she's just not in the mood. She puts the book back as the steward shoves the refreshment cart towards her.

'Drink, madam?' he asks. She decides she shouldn't, then that she should. She asks for red and is given a plastic tumbler and a miniature bottle of something called Exotic Nights, with a picture of a man and a woman clinking glasses on a harbour at sunset. Are harbours exotic? Perhaps in Monaco or somewhere like that, which, judging by the picture, it looks like the manufacturers are trying to evoke. Less so in Aberdeen, where she's from. The steward looks at her neighbour, opens his mouth, then shrugs, kicks the trolley brake up and moves on, wrinkling his nose once more.

She sips the wine. She could use this wine to de−limescale her bathroom. She screws the top back on the bottle and sighs, glancing to her left just in time to see the man's drool splat onto his shirt.

Somewhere towards the front of the plane, a baby wails then stops. Debbie looks at her fellow passengers. Most are watching movies. Others, like her neighbour, are sleeping. Maybe she should do the same, if she can ignore the ketchup stink.

Debbie spends the next hour and a half with her eyes firmly closed, not sleeping a wink. Then there's a rumble. Her eyes blink open and the seatbelt light pops on. They're landing. She fastens herself in and her stomach jumps as the plane drops from the sky. Her ears pop. The man is still asleep. Her heart pounds as the wheels touch the runway and the plane, just for a split second, feels as if it might career off the tarmac and hurtle into a nearby building. A part of her hopes it does. But it doesn't. Instead it slows and slows and slows and … stops. The seatbelt light flashes off again and she unbuckles her seatbelt as people around her clamber to their feet. The Greek sunshine streams through the windows. The man stirs, blinks, opens his eyes, yawns and stretches.

'I must have fallen asleep,' he says. 'Are we there?' Debbie nods. Yes, we're there.

He leans in to kiss her. The smell is so overpowering she holds her breath while he shoves his lips against hers. 'Then let's get this honeymoon started!'

She looks into his face and knows with iron certainty that she's made a big mistake.

'Yes, let's,' she says.

Fair, Unfair

Georgia Cook

"Where are you going?" asked the wolf, with his gleaming eyes and his glossy—black fur. "You've come through the woods already, and you're so close to Grandmother's house."

The little girl in the red cape shrugged. There was moss in her hair, and smudges of dirt on both cheeks. The basket in her arms was grubby and worn.

"Back home," she said.

"Back home?"

"Oh yes," the little girl nodded. "Or that way."

She pointed in a direction neither had been before, off into the shadows beyond the path. She rustled as she moved; briars had wound themselves into her cloak, sticking up through the fabric like porcupine quills.

"Why?" asked the wolf. "That's not how the story's supposed to go; *you* follow the path and I follow *you*. We must all abide by the narrative."

The little girl shook her head.

"Not this time," she said. "I've been thinking, you see, and I've decided it's not fair."

The wolf flashed white fangs. His ears twitched.

"Fair?" he sneered. "Why should a fairytale be *fair*? It's never been fair before."

The little girl glared.

"It isn't fair for *me*, and it isn't fair for *you*, so it isn't fair. Neither of us asked to be a metaphor; whether I wanted to be eaten, or if you wanted to eat. It was simply *decided*."

"Well, yes," said the wolf, with the agonising patience of a predator. "Because I am a wolf and you are a little girl, and if I do not attempt to eat you, how will anyone learn?"

"I think they can learn for themselves," she said. "Or tell a different story, one with a clearer point. I'm done with it all."

She straightened her shoulders, lifted her chin.

"I will choose what I want to do, and I want to walk through the woods."

The wolf looked from the little girl to the blackness between the trees. There is little to fear from the woods, when one has always been the wolf, but much to fear in the sudden loss of one's certainty. "What if you find something worse than me out there?" he asked. "A bigger monster? A nastier story? What will you do then? You don't *know*."

"Then that will be *my* decision, and *my* story, and *I'll* choose what I make of it," said the little girl, picking the moss from her hair. "Maybe I'll come back, maybe I won't. Perhaps you'll find something better to do. Who knows?"

And with that, she dropped her red cloak, kicked her basket into the bracken, and headed off into the gloom.

In search of another story. Or another wolf. Or simply something different.

Bees

Judy Upton

There's a bee buzzing against the window. My eyes keep drifting up as it pushes itself angrily at the grimy glass. I think it wonders why it can see the light but never reach it. If I could, I'd get up and let it out, but leaving my workstation really isn't worth the hassle that would cause me. They fine you for everything here. A minute late in the morning, too long in the toilet or getting a cup of water – whatever.

Dust sparkles in the air, and the machines whirr in your ears night and day. Anala who sits in front of me is coughing. If she's sick she still won't go home. There's no pay if you're ill at home, but there's rent and bills and mouths to feed no matter what.

I'm inserting a mesh panel into the front of a sparkly top. It's the kind of thing a young girl might wear in a nightclub, but there aren't any clubs open now, so why are we even making it? I know there are illegal parties, but haven't people enough things in their wardrobe? Why don't they get us making protective clothes for doctors and nurses instead? If I was doing something like that, it wouldn't be so bad. The bee's in the same situation. It should be outside collecting honey for its family. Instead it's stuck in here struggling up and down a small pane of glass as I guide my needle up and down this piece of cloth. If someone swatted the bee, would anyone back at the hive or wherever it lives miss it? My family would miss me if I died here, but no one else would really notice. A woman, late last year, fainted on the floor. It was just after midday and by three o'clock someone else was sitting at her sewing machine completing the skirt she was making. Busy like a bee, then swatted, and gone.

If this place and the other factories closed though, where would we go? How would we live? On my way home I often look in the windows of shops and cafés and I used to think 'I'd like to work there'. Because you see people walking by. And you don't get fined for chatting, as far as I know.

Now, places are only just starting to open again, and some of them still have their shutters down. Maybe some of them won't come back.

I've heard there are long queues at the Job Centre now. I went there once, but they said, "You've got a job already." I said it doesn't even pay the minimum wage. "Well, it should do," the man said. "That's the law."

"And how am I supposed to make them obey that law?" I asked him.

"Join a union. Go on strike." I tried to explain. In my job you can't join a union, there are no strikes, you're either working or you aren't.

"You do have the right to work here legally?" the Job Centre man said. He was looking at my National Insurance number. It was right there in front of him. I had to fill it in on a form before I even got to see him. He was wearing a rugby shirt under his suit jacket. It had stripes on it. Orange and black like a bee. I think our company might have made it. We did a lot of rugby shirts last year. I remember seeing one in a sports

177

store when I went to buy our two their football kit for school. I couldn't believe the price.

If I went to the market, bought the material and made the shirts myself, I'd make a profit. I could do it from home on a second–hand sewing machine. I even asked in one of the smaller shops, if they'd want to stock some shirts and tops if I made them. The woman said no. They already had their suppliers. I asked her how much she paid her supplier for each shirt. She wouldn't tell me. Her shop is shuttered now. I don't know if she's going to re–open.

I think everyone buys their clothes online anyway. Would it be any use trying to sell things through a website? Would anyone see my little webpage with a few items on it?

It would be a big risk to set up my own business if I had to give up this job to do it. How do you start something up when you've nothing to spend?

When I come in from work I can't face more sewing. I have to soak my fingers in salt water to soften the hard skin and soothe the cracks and blisters. How do I find time to make items to sell?

The bee has stopped buzzing. It's sitting quietly on the windowsill now. It's learnt that escape is hopeless. It has accepted its fate. It will spend its last minutes or hours in this hot, airless place. For the bee, the memories of flowers – their beauty, their colours and their perfumes are fading. Anala is coughing again. "It's so hot!" she says.

My supervisor is at the other end of the room, by the fire–escape door, trying to get a phone signal. I dart across to the window. I unlatch it and push it open a little. I know there are no flowers outside, just concrete, brick and rubbish down below. But as I return to my machine the bee has crawled towards the crack. I can feel fresh air on my face, but as soon as my supervisor realises the window is open he will close it again. The bee has only a short time to gain enough strength to crawl outside. I find myself whispering, 'Go on, bee. Go.'

Fun Quiz!!! How Well Do You Know Your Dad?

Anne Howkins

You're on a family holiday, somewhere in Cornwall. The sea air has cleared your skin and your hair is sun−streaked. Only a few days now till you let Simon loose on your golden body. Dad asks you if you want to drive to that beach in the brochure for a walk. Why do you go?

- a) To spend quality time together, been ages since it was just you and Dad!
- b) It's better than being left in charge of the little ones so Mum and Dad can have a nap (sex) in the afternoons…
- c) You need to talk about school, Jenny and Karen are evil bitches. Mum never has time to listen.

The beach is endless. Marram grass murmurs as your feet slip− slide through shifting sand dunes. The sea is so far away it seems like sky. Do you talk to Dad?

a) Yes! He has some great ideas about handling Jenny and Karen! And he says Simon's a good lad, he's so happy you've found a perfect boyfriend!

b) You start to, Dad asks some questions, but nothing too deep. He's never been good at talking about emotional stuff. He says he'll do something with the little ones, so you get time to chat with Mum, she'll know the answer.

c) No, he's still raging at fucking idiots not knowing how to reverse into passing places. The ebbing tide steals your voice.

Running to the sea, breathless slapping through wet sand, you race as if that's all there is in the world. Is this fun?

a) Yes! Dad lets you win and swings you through the waves like he does with the little ones!

b) Maybe. Dad is out of breath halfway. He thinks you don't know about his secret ciggies.

c) No. Dad treats everything like a competition he must win. He splashes you with freezing cold seawater. At least it washes away your tears.

As you sift for treasure at the high—water mark, Dad slips a handful of sea glass nuggets into your sandy fists. How long will you keep this gift?

a) Forever, stored in your memory box! When you hold them, you will remember the closeness you shared!

b) They will turn up every time you move house, which will be often. Simon will give them back to you at a mediation meeting.

c) You will leave them in the holiday cottage.

Your stomach clocks drag you back to the car park. Dad hands you the map saying, *You're getting us back to the cottage.* What happens?

a) He ruffles your hair and kisses your cheek when you get back to the cottage, saying *That's my clever girl!!!*

b) You realise you've told him to turn right not left. You both laugh when he says he's going to get R and L tattooed on your hands.

c) You stare at the map. Roads wriggle like snakes, hissing misdirection. He stops at a crossroads, leaving rubber on tarmac, and a ribbon of steely smoke. Saltwater stains the map as he spins the car around in a U–turn that leaves your stomach churning for hours.

How did you do?

Mainly a)   Wow, we're so jealous, you've got a great dad! We bet your friends think so too.

Mainly b)   Sounds pretty normal to us! Don't stop talking to him and remember to tell him how much you love him!

Mainly c)   Maybe one day he'll look back and see what an arse he's been. Just don't count on it.

Sexercise

Corey Miller

Kimberly doesn't like to eat before we have sex, says it makes her feel pregnant. It's become a workout for her, scheduled gym time to drop fat. We do different positions in front of the full—length mirror to stretch out our *rectus femoralis* with twenty repetitions in each stance. Missionary has become too stationary so to please Kimberly we switch to others: reverse cowgirl, wheelbarrow, pile driver, and finish with a move I think she invented called The Flying Squirrel — all to burn more calories. I didn't care much to lose weight and stay active, but you take it when you can get it.

She counts each thrust out loud and her dirty talk has become: *Keep going, Push harder, Is that all you got?* She yells at me like we're training for something. The music she plays is two generations before us and I have a tough time cumming because all I can picture is Richard Simmons *Sweatin' to the Oldies.* We continue through the motions until I have to fake it and discard the rubber immediately. She does a standing backflip then karate chops my mahogany desk, telling me to NEVER throw out her protein shake.

Kimberly starts to add more weight and resistance — straps and dumbbells. I can't tell if penetration exists anymore. Gluten no longer does. We hopped on a paleo cleanse and eat carnivorous: Slim Jims and raw bacon.

I've been seeing odd shapes and getting hard. Pull—up diapers make me think of working out and I get a raging hard—on wanting to uppercut out of my pants like the Kool—Aid man — Oh Yeah. Kimberly doesn't want kids though and I don't blame her. I wouldn't want to push a life—form out of a sphincter around people I just met while leaking bodily fluids. I mention this to her and somehow it redirects her alignment, like she was balance beaming on the fence. She now thinks it's the ultimate form of exercise. I think she just wants to gain weight so she'll have something to lose.

We workout — a.k.a. The Sex — and I go to pull out, but she has me wrapped like an MFA fighter grappling on the mat, choking me and she won't let me tap out. Her thighs are as thick as telephone poles.

I ask my boss if I can stop working from home.

Now Kimberly is Prego like the pasta sauce we eat on carb day before her triathlons. Even with a bigger belly she maintains eight—pack abs.

I get scared watching her do backhand springs into a reverse 4.5 somersault from the pike position off the high dive. *I'm a Trophy Wife*, she says from atop of the podium.

Her water breaks and it's all Blue Powerade, full of electrolytes. In the delivery room, she does chin—ups for 20 hours until the baby drops out.

The baby emerges and Kimberly curls it, a thousand reps at 6.4 ounces. I think she was hoping to be some Octomom and shoot them out like a bazooka, as if birthing only one is a sign of weakness. Although, delivering the baby after only 6 months of pregnancy makes her feel special and better than the other moms. She names the baby Medal, spit shines it, and puts it up on the shelf.

I supervise Medal while Kimberly records herself flexing with Vaseline glazing her like the donuts I can't have. I don't even drink beer for fear of calorie shame, yet, I have a beer belly. Maybe I'm getting pregnant now.

She wants enough children to set the record for juggling objects. I try and call it "Making Love" but that's something you do when it's slow and passionate. This is Fucking. I'm no longer a giving person and am now like the butt of a joke, on the receiving end. She rides me like a stationary bike training for marathons. She stands on me as her surfboard, but it's dry AF. She uses my nuts for speed bag practice. I never pegged her as the gym rat type when we began dating, but I want to be supporting like the bras she no longer needs with only muscle rocks for boobs; at least I have use for her old WonderBras. As soon as she finishes with me, she dangles Medal around her neck and cartwheels out of the bedroom.

Kimberly participates in the LA Marathon and breaks out ahead of the pack. She started in the back and trampled over everything in her way. She's twice the speed of anyone in the race. She's so fast she can't slow down and turn to follow the course. She sprints straight out of the city, onto the beach, and runs on water into the Pacific Ocean. Her body shrinks as she travels off into the distance. Usually races circle back to the starting point to finish but she keeps going and going and going and …

A Different View

Emma Robertson

The table is set for three but Jenny hasn't yet arrived. Nonetheless, Mum cannot resist pouring the champagne, rather fizzing with excitement herself. The bubbles froth into elegant coupe glasses; trendily vintage, or should I say classic? The sort you'd stack high in a pyramid for a champagne fountain, like Matt and I joked we would have at our wedding reception.

I admire the crisp white linen tablecloth, the silverware, the fine china plates. We could have met anywhere, but Mum insisted we celebrate and so here we are on the terrace of a rather lovely hotel, just across the river from the new apartment. If you crane your neck you can almost see the building from here.

I reach for my champagne glass and promptly knock it to the floor. The glass smashes onto the stone tiles and heads turn in our direction. "Sorry," I say to Mum.

"No problem, no problem, don't worry!" she faffs, already out of her chair and scooping up the larger pieces of broken glass. I notice the waiting staff looking uncomfortable, wearing the same wary expressions they had when they saw us arrive. After an uncertain pause the head waiter approaches with a dustpan and brush. "I'm so sorry," Mum says to him.

He bats away her apologies and sweeps up the remaining debris with impressive speed. This is clearly not his first coupe catastrophe.

"Shall I bring another glass?" he addresses Mum rather than me. "Or would you prefer something … sturdier?"

I feel the embarrassment oozing out of him. No one knows how to act around me anymore. Generally, as now, they simply ignore me and talk to Mum instead.

"Another glass will be fine, thank you. I'll help her," Mum adds, when the waiter hesitates.

She smiles at me as he shuffles off. I wouldn't say she is enjoying this, not at all; she has only recently stopped bursting into tears whenever she looks at me. However, there is certainly a part of her that is flourishing as a result of being needed again.

Jenny's arrival breaks the silence. Mum greets her with a hug, asking after Jenny's little boy. "Is Daddy babysitting today?"

To anyone else Jenny would insist that a father looking after his own son was parenting, not babysitting, but she won't talk to my mum like that, so instead she just nods and reaches over to give me a hug. She is nervous, I know, partly because of what she has just done but partly because she's scared to touch me these days.

She sits down and tucks a shiny black curl behind her ear, before it immediately escapes, and she tucks it behind her ear again. It reminds me of when we were girls and she taught me how to braid it in neat rows. She wears it naturally now, which is good because a, it suits her and b, there's no way I would have the fine motor skills to help her braid it these days.

"So, how did it go?" I ask her as Mum pours her a glass of fizz. My replacement glass hasn't arrived yet so Mum fills my water glass instead and holds it to my lips.

Jenny hesitates. I know that she is one of the few people who can understand my speech, so this pause must be because she doesn't want to answer.

"Was she there?" I press. Jenny sighs and nods.

"Brazen cow," Mum mutters.

Jenny bites her lip and I feel sorry for asking her to help until I remember that she knew about Allie and Matt for almost two months before she made them come clean. "Tell me."

"I've got the rest of your stuff in the car; that was no problem," she begins, pausing as the waiter places a tiered cake stand on the table and explains to Mum and Jenny what each delectable item is. As he retreats, Jenny takes a scone and starts crumbling it absentmindedly. "Allie has already moved in. She wanted me to say to you again that ... that she's sorry. That they both are."

I fight the urge to send another glass to floor, on purpose this time. It's just such a cliché for my best friend and my fiancé to have had an affair whilst I was laid up in hospital recovering from the accident. And for my other best friend to help cover it up. I'm almost as angry about their lack of imagination as I am about the betrayal.

"Forget about them," says Mum, waving her hand as if shooing away a fly. As if it is that easy to forget two of the most important people in my life. As if I'd ever be able to trust anyone again.

As if anyone would want me now anyway.

"So, is everything all signed and sealed on the new place?" Jenny looks me right in the eye, imploring me to go with her on the change of subject. She's trying hard to make amends and I do appreciate the fact that she always talks directly to me, not over my head like so many people do now. She sees past the power chair, the permanent spasms and slurred speech. She sees that I'm still here. Inside.

I nod as Mum fills her in on the high ceilings and beautiful river view, the clever ramp access that means I'll be able to get in and out independently even if the lift conks out. The fact that there's plenty of room for her to move in with me to start with, "Just until you're on your feet!" Mum titters, before freezing in horror at her own turn of phrase. Jenny meets my eye and grins. I can't help but smile too.

"It's great to use your compensation from the accident to get such a cool place," she says, raising her glass. "A new start."

"A new start!" Mum echoes.

She holds the glass to my lips and I drink.

How My Best Friend Helped Me Grieve My Family

Anika Carpenter

Red felt pens always ran out the quickest, so I wrote my list in green instead; jammy dodgers, maraschino cherries, raspberry jelly, craft paper, strawberries and Kit Kats. I added red and black icing, because my big sister, Manon, said she'd make me a ladybird cake. I reckoned the whole lot wouldn't cost more than ten pounds. I'd saved fifteen. Mum was pleased with my plans. A red birthday party would coordinate with the made–to–order Liberty curtains, the De'Longhi coffee machine, and her Max Mara dress, the one she likes to whip out of reach of my 'grotesque little fingers'.

I taught myself to make paper roses. They were to decorate the garden, because 'indoors is for grown–up parties'. I stayed up past midnight for three nights so that there were enough. If I hadn't, Dad would've gone up into the loft and got the Christmas tinsel down. He'd have laughed as he wrapped it around tree branches and the legs of garden furniture, but I'd cringe because it reminds me of hairy oak caterpillars and how once he told me that their toxic hairs were as 'soft as bunny's tails' and I chose to believe him.

The kids from my class looked so cool. Daniel Levin came dressed as Spider–Man; the new girl, Susan, came as The Queen of Hearts; John Logan was a lobster and my best friend, Lena, came wrapped in the Swedish flag. Dad put on some of Mum's 'Cherry Dream' lipstick, played 'The Lady In Red' too loudly and tried to get us all to dance. Mum caught him and ushered us into the garden, 'Out, out, go have your party, you have an hour and a half.'

Manon didn't make a cake. My friends sang round a stale Victoria sponge which had 'had a yellow sticker on it'. Instead of candles and icing, there was squirty cream and a tangle of strawberry shoelaces. Before the singing finished most of it had slopped on to the floor like cat's guts. Lena held my hand and said, 'We'll move to Sweden when we're grown–ups. I'll buy you Princess Cake for breakfast, lunch and dinner and we'll have a garden with fruit trees and real roses growing up and over the brick wall.'

Brown Piano

Christopher Pham

The ivories at my fingertips; I've nearly forgotten this feeling. One and two and three and four and, I count to myself; you're making me nervous. My hands tremble as I approach you for the first time, in what feels like a lifetime. We begin Chopin's *Winter Wind*. I know a thousand apologies could never make up for what I've done — don't worry, I swear I'll make it up to you.

I pour my every breath and emotion onto you, it's finally time — **FORTE**. A cascade of flying notes fills the entirety of my soul? I don't hold back and you don't either. I pour more and more emotion, more than I have; it's worth it.

I experience every part of your body as if you're an extension of myself, and you respond with indulgent pleasure. During our youth we were inseparable. Other kids ran around and played, yet I only wanted to spend time with you. Through the good and the bad, you were always there.

Now that I've lost everything, I've returned to you. I'm ignoring the wrong I've done, and I'm sorry. Again, a thousand apologies can't make up for it.

How can you understand, when I don't deserve your understanding? I've hurt you and treated you like you were nothing. Why do you care for me?

I continue with the etude, desperately trying to make things right. It may be possible for things to be right with you – but with myself is the rub. I've come back to you now that I have nothing. *You don't care.*

Do you remember the last time we were together? I've said things that I can't take back, and left pitiful tears behind. I remember that lonely summer day; I always spent entire summers with you. Other people just couldn't understand me like you could. They called me names, breaking me until I felt like nothing – maybe I really was nothing. Yet, I left you. Was it out of anger, sadness, or maybe both? I used the excuse of shame to never apologize. It took me too many years to realize the parasitic nature of any other attachment.

This new wind is approaching the world, one only you and I can feel. As I listen to its subtlety, I hear the words, "I love you." I love you even if I hate you. I love you even if you're the cause of my suffering. I love you even if you isolate me.

I'm at my final push, it'll be all that's left of me. One day we'll equally lose each other – ***marcatissimo***. These are the final measures; the final, permanent step that'll be tattooed onto what's left of my character.

The song ends its final notes, and water drips over these old ivory keys. Why am I suddenly crying? I look over at the engagement ring that lays on top of this brown piano.

I deserved to lose this woman, but I still miss her. All I can do is say it one last time,

"I love you, and I'm sorry."

Forever After?

Jennifer Thrall

She didn't belong here.

It was supposed to be the happiest day of her life.

Confetti in her hair, flowers adorning each table and doorway, a cacophony of celebration.

Head heavy, she had walked down the aisle and recited her vows in a fog. The white dress encasing her body was tight, squeezing the air out of her lungs.

She caught the eye of her new husband across the room and attempted a weak smile.

So caught up in the excitement of planning and organising, she hadn't really thought about the commitment, the responsibility, the forever after. It wasn't that he was a bad man; he was lovely, dependable, kind. She cared for him deeply; but was that enough for forever?

Her chest tightened and her head spun. The fog closed in on her, like choking smoke. Smiling faces, uttering words of congratulations swirled passed her as she pushed through the crowd of well-wishers. She burst through the doors, and breathed deeply, the cool air filling her lungs. Across the lawn the dark trees of the woods called to her.

She kicked off her ridiculous white shoes and ran. She clawed at the suffocating dress, ripping the buttons open and letting it fall to the ground.

She ran into the woods in the lacy, white underwear she had chosen for her wedding night. Her head lifted, her shoulders relaxed and an enormous rush of freedom came over her. She knew that she could never return.

They're Waiting

Anna Ross

I tightened my grip on my gun. Pressure dug into my fingers. My hands shook. Tiny flakes of snow fell slowly into the wet mud. I heard faint screams up ahead; screams and gunshots. It was only a matter of time before they broke through our defences, there were just so many of them.

The thud of bullets died away. Snarls and cries echoed into silence. I looked at my partner. He had the look I had seen in so many others. The moment had finally come.

I could see my breath on the air. My heart was hammering in my chest.

Three… two… one… CRASH!

I jumped backwards as an unseen force smashed into the barricade. Heaving like a living entity, it groaned as the enemy piled up against it, grasping to force it open.

I raised my gun and fired my first shot. Aimed at a grotesque hand bursting through the rotting woodwork. I don't know if it hit. My eardrums rang as the entire battalion started shooting.

The walls were being torn apart. I saw faces emerge through gaps, twisted rabid faces rotting right off the body. Each one howling through bloodstained teeth like animals. They were mad and… so hungry…

"Alex."

They were breaking through…

"Alex, take that silly thing off."

The world disappeared before my eyes and I was back in my living room. I blinked. No snow, no struggle, just soft blue carpet and yellow walls covered in *Star Wars* posters. My mother was looking down at me, my VR headset in her hand.

"Alex, I've been calling for ages. Come and help set the table, it's teatime."

"Oh, come on Mum, just five minutes: the zombies were about to—"

"I don't care what was going to happen. It's lasagne and we're not letting it go cold."

I had a far greater chance of killing zombies than winning an argument with Mum.

"Fine," I muttered, putting the plastic gun down on my bed and pausing the game. "Suppose I'll just have to save the world later."

No Regrets

James FitzGibbon

'I never have any regrets,' Mohamed said, leaning back. 'We do things according to how we feel. We are, how you say, pre–programmed?'

Daphne, the class teacher, had invited a group of students out to this restaurant in the *Souq* for a conversation class. The girls she wanted to come couldn't make it, so she felt a little vulnerable being the only woman with a group of five men. But, as she was a professional, she did not make this known, setting her chin in defiance. This class in particular had proved to be a challenge. She felt animosity tinged with disappointment from the males that she was female. This had gone back to day one and, despite her working hard to produce interesting learning materials, that feeling had never really subsided. She felt the young men were arrogant, acting like they were looking down at her.

'You couldn't really blame them,' she thought to herself, as they had been brought up to see women as inferior. Nannies had looked after them as small children and they and their brothers and male family had told them what to do. These nannies were usually older Filipina women, brought in to leave the parents free to do whatever they liked, depriving kids of parental love and guidance.

To make matters worse, Daphne was young and attractive.

'So, if you have no regrets, do you believe in Fate?' Daphne asked.

Arif, looking down his nose and raising an eyebrow, explained.

'You see, teacher, it is God's will. *Insh'Allah*. We say this. It means 'If God wills it'. We are only his children. He tells us what to do.'

'Like your homework,' said Daphne, chuckling. 'If God doesn't want you to do it, as is often the case, then it doesn't get done'.

The men, not seeing the intended funny side of this remark, sighed.

'You Americans,' said Mohamed, 'you think you can come over here and teach us your ways. "Do this by this day, do that by then." Well: it just doesn't work. You are here, Miss Daphne, only to help us with our English. Nothing more. You cannot create little Americans here. If *Allah* wants us to go in another way that stops us from doing homework, then you must understand.'

'No', said Daphne, her hands under the table, tearing up a paper serviette.

After an uncomfortable silence, she said:

'I'm not sure you understand. I'm trying to train you to meet the expectations of University. I'm telling you: if you say *'Insh'Allah'* to one of the doctors when they give you an assignment, and it doesn't get done, do you think it'll be understood? Do you think you'll be successful? Do you think you won't be dismissed?'

They all sighed. It felt like an Eternity before someone broke the silence.

'Our fathers are rich men,' said Saad, another student in the group, his eyes half–lidded and playing with his prayer beads. 'We learn English because one day we will take over their businesses. We will do this soon. We have no time to go abroad to study. If we need M.B.A., then we pay someone to do it here. If we need Ph.D., then we pay. Nothing's free. Every–body accepts that.'

'But have you never experienced the joy and integrity of learning? Believe me: there's nothing like it!'

'What you say teacher?' said Arif. 'Only you Americans can afford to be like this. You walk around this Earth thinking you are better than everyone else. We have to work. We have no time for this joy of learning. We have many things to pay for.'

He spread his arms wide. 'Do you think all this is free? Just for your enjoyment? We build this from nothing. This lovely *Souq* is made nice for you. All the parks you enjoy: we need to bring water to feed the grass on the sand. And we need to import the trees. Nothing happens here without money.'

Daphne had heard all this before. On top of that, she was the teacher, who was meant to be controlling this meeting, and not these arrogant young men.

'Forgive me for saying. It is you with the Maseratis,' she said. 'You with the Rolex watches. As teachers, we don't earn that much. I cannot afford these things.'

Mohamed, who had been listening to this conversation, laughed out loud, throwing his head back. Then he leaned forward, became very serious and looked Daphne in the eye.

'Why you come, then?' he said. 'If you don't like it here, go somewhere else. The world is – how you say? – your oyster. You are free. We will not stop you!'

Everyone looked embarrassed, making no eye contact. One stared at the table in front of him, some looked at their hands, others pulled out their mobiles.

'There are many things I like here. The Corniche is just amazing. And the museums! And the night-life and bars! You understand why many people come here.'

'So,' said Arif. 'You drink alcohol. You know it is forbidden here.'

'It's normal where I come from.'

'You know,' said Mohamed, glaring with eyes full of malice, 'a teacher should be virtuous. Free from addictions. I admire this. Being taught by a drunken privileged woman is not something I like.'

The other men sat back in their seats. One coughed.

Mohamed smiled.

'You are, though,' he said, almost like it was a consolation prize, 'a good-looking woman.'

Daphne fought back her emotions. She said, eyes glistening, 'Do you enjoy being cruel? Do you have no regrets being so inhospitable to the guests of your country?'

Mohamed sensed he had overdone it. He had been very outspoken about his beliefs. And, for a moment, felt guilty for mistreating his teacher. He leant back again, snorting. He was unsmiling.

Then, almost, as if a light had been switched on somewhere, he said, raising his chin:

'Like I said, I don't regret anything.'

My Favourite Husband

Gemma Al−Khayat

'Do you find it *weird* living with someone else?' Lorraine asks in a low voice.

What she's really asking, I think, is whether I feel guilty. I choose my answer carefully, not wishing to be disloyal.

'I don't think he'd have wanted me to be on my own forever.'

'No. Of course he wouldn't,' Lorraine agrees with a dismissive wave of her hand. 'It's probably stranger for us because we're not used to seeing you with someone else.'

My 50th had seemed an appropriate opportunity for Alan to meet everyone and get all the awkward introductions out of the way. As I watch him shuffling around the room, the only one not dressed in jeans, I am embarrassed by his discomfort and impatient that he can't relax. But then I see the tense, closed−lipped smiles of our friends when he tries to talk to them and watch as they whisper together behind his departing back, 'not at all what I was expecting' and 'very different'. After that, I stop blaming him for not being you.

Sometimes I wonder what you would have thought of Alan. I know he's not a 'man's man' like you and he'll never be the life and soul of any party. But it can't be easy sharing me with you. And I'll always be grateful to him for picking me up off the floor where I had lain in a broken heap for so long.

Lying in bed tonight, my back is so tense I'm sure I must be levitating. Alan stirs and, realising I can't sleep, reaches out to take my hand. Instantly I am transported back to that vast night when, sitting beside your hospital bed, I felt your hand slowly turning cold in mine. But here and now my hand is in the hand of another, and Alan's is warm.

Longtime whatever, first time blah

Isabel Thompson

I greet Soel off the ferry with a two–armed hug. She barrels forward, squeezing the living guts out of me. It's her first time off the island in months and right now the rest of the passengers' stares don't mean a thing. We hold each other ferociously.

She pulls back to read my face. "So what happened?"

"Huh?"

"The text. I was so worried."

"Oh… nah dude. It's nothing."

"Bullshit."

I look down at her hair rather than her eyes. The roots have grown out almost an inch since we dyed it, the ends still bleach blonde.

I'm hugging her. I don't know what to say.

She places a hand on my arm.

"Shall I get us a cuppa?"

"Aye. I need it."

Whilst she's away getting the drinks I sit on the edge of the pier, picking pebbles out of the concrete and dropping them into the bay. My phone weighs so heavy in my pocket. I consider letting it slide out and splash down below, but stories of conflict minerals and child labour hold me back.

"Cheer up love," I hear behind me. It's a running joke from Soel's last visit when some drunk cunts told us to smile more, and we told them where to go.

She sits next to me on the concrete edge. We dangle our legs into the space beyond, watching a group of jellyfish pulsating in a square of green water lit up by sun.

"Out with it, woman!"

I give in.

"I submitted a poem and I lied."

She waits for more, then:

"And?"

"Well, I never expected them to get back to me, did I? I thought I'd be getting an email like four months from now with a generic *sorry not this time* reply."

"But they got back to you?"

"Yeah, they got back to me. That's the problem. I started it off with the fake—happy jaunty and totally false opener: *hi, longtime reader, first time submitting.* It's just a fucking phrase. I didn't think they'd even respond, let alone *care.*"

Soel crunches up her face and lights a cigarette. I'm trying to quit but I poach the tobacco pouch from her lap.

"Jesus, I thought someone had died," she mutters, "can we please have a code word to discern genuine freak—outs in future?"

"Dude this *is* genuine. I finally had the balls to share this thing, I sent it as far away as I possibly could in the English—speaking world, and now everything is fucked because they think I read all their stuff."

Something clicks.

"Is this why you asked if my mum had any Australian poetry mags you could borrow?"

"Yeah."

"She doesn't by the way, but even if she did, I don't think she'd lend you any till you give her Meg Bateman back."

I love that book. "Fine. It's on my desk."

She looks at her phone. "What time we going to the boat?"

"About now. I'm such a fucking numpty, Soel."

"Aye," she says. "That you are."

On the bus I ignore her. I'm scrolling through a catalogue of back issues and trying to decide which to get. This could be a very expensive lie.

"You only have to get two or three, right? Just lie your arse off more and say these are your favourites."

I exhale behind my COVID mask and my glasses fog up.

"I don't want to, but the only other option is to tell them I'm full of shit."

I click on three that jump off the screen at me with their titles. Three elements I can relate to.

She spends the bus ride looking out at the wizened oaks and coppiced hazel trees in full leaf, the loch running parallel to the road, the greylag geese she might see at the turning just before Fearnoch forest. I've seen these things nearly every day for the past two months, on my way to work on the shell of a boat that I'm supposed to be living on in three weeks' time.

This time, I read stories from the south side of the globe.

★

They're actually really good. No actually about it. Really good.

I think about what my life would've been like if I'd read these when they were first published.

We're busy at the boat today. Soel is wobbly clambering up the ladder the first time but gets the hang of it. We drag a tin of paint down, some overalls, and some brushes I found in a skip, and get to work. I spend the morning lying in cool shade underneath the hull, slapping on primer for the antifouling. Stripping it back to the gelcoat has taken a solid month of scraping, cursing, sweating.

It's hard going but the space between the twin keels keeps me shielded from the sun and I lie with my hair tangled in seaweed, in this womblike space, thinking of the past.

When the tide chases us in and we can work no more, we sit on deck waiting for the kettle to boil. I read some more and compose my lie whilst she rolls and smokes, and rolls again.

"Let's see!" she leans in and tucks her chin over my shoulder.

"I've gotten this far," and I read my reply.

"*Thanks so much for getting back to me! I used to get old copies off my dad's neighbour – the most meaningful of these to me was the misfit volume. It was so powerful for me, as a young person, to read about people's experiences with being ostracised, mental health issues, feeling like you don't belong. I didn't have many other channels where I could find people expressing all this pain in creative work – the poetry we read at school was all from a different time and I couldn't relate to any of it.*"

"Bit mushy," she considers, "but a lot of it's the truth."

"Aye… well."

"What was the poem about anyway?"

"You know how I dropped out a year early?"

She nods and hugs me tight.

"Basically that."

Fuck it. I just press send.

The weekend passes and Soel's returned to her island. It's so rainy I can't see it on the horizon for curtains of cloud. It's so rainy that the boat just sits, fifteen miles away, and there's fuck all I can do to it in this weather. The sealant's gone in the windows again.

I'm stewing away in bed in the room I sublet off the guy who's coming back in three weeks. There's nothing for it. I check my email.

My head spirals into a dwam.

They know.

They saw the eBook downloads from Scotland. They know I'm a liar.

The waves of latent guilt roll in.

I cry for a bit.

Not about the email but for the past. I'm not sad about the email itself, just angry at my own stupidity. I never should have done it this way.

There's stuff that I never tell people.

I never really told Soel the full story.

I don't know what I'm doing here, stuck being sad about stuff that happened years ago. There's nothing to do about it now.

I peel my head off the soggy pillow and clamber over boxes to my desk to write a reply.

The first part is my response to their critique of the poem. It's actually helpful in an annoying way and points out where the rhythm tails off. I offer my edits and justifications.

The second half, I entitle: *With regards to falsity*, and come clean.

In closure: *Freaked out that someone actually responded, I did the obvious dumb thing. On the plus side I genuinely enjoyed reading those three issues.*

I write poems for me and my trauma. Trauma fucks with your rhythms.

Sorry not sorry.

Then I sign my name and climb back under the duvet.

I wake up some time later with a dehydration headache.

The bastard's responded.

I expect some kind of lofty spiel that lying your way into the literary world was a big no-no (duh). What I read is a surprisingly measured and human response. And more surprising still, they ask me to write about it all; the emails, everything.

I hate their kindness. It feels like a trap.

But I still find myself scribbling stuff down in the notebook I keep in my bed.

I can feel the gunk trapped inside trying to flush itself out. One way or another, it needs to be processed.

Boob Jobs

Andrea Tate

Looking back, you realize this shit started in the 4th grade at Waterford Elementary. Waterford was a public school, your first public school. Before then you attended Catholic schools that mostly focused on Jesus. No one talked about anatomy unless it had to do with bleeding palms and feet. You were clueless about the little raised bumps developing on your chest. What job did they serve?

In fifth grade, the math teacher stares. The boy sitting in front of you stares. The boy sitting in back of you wants a better view to stare. Your girlfriends are jealous, while you envy their androgynous figures. You begin to hate these bulbous new visitors. At this age, you just want to fit in, not stand out. It is likely you don't even know too much about sex. You may only know differentiation. He is a boy. You are a girl. We are different sexes, so don't bug me.

At fourteen, these no-good things have to come with you to your first job. You are working at the local bakery with your best friend. She is lucky because she doesn't have any noticeable front appendages. But you, on the other hand, get cupcake frosting in the worst places. Those bakery shelves aren't meant to compete with a human shelf. The owner is a sweet old Polish man who probably has granddaughters your age. He tries to help you out one day by telling you your uniform is too tight and you should probably get the next size up. In the end, your bakery job proves to be a challenge because you truly can't stop eating free donuts and muffins, and now, baby not only has front, she has back.

The worst part, is men seem to think that these two vessels are actually advertising an invitation for sex. Big boobs seem to be a neon sign flashing, "I'm here for your pleasure. Come fuck me. Come one, come all." However, things change at sixteen when you start working as a waitress at a local Greek diner. You start to see the bigger the boobs, the bigger the tips. You realize you can make these things pay for all the suffering they have caused you thus far. You begin to use them. It is a secret agreement on a "look but don't touch" policy. You notice your male customers look at your chest while giving you their order; cooks make your food before they make your male co-workers', bosses stand a little too close for comfort. You serve people food. They ogle at your chest and pay you for the favor.

College brings a new set of challenges. You are now an adult. It is legal for men to touch your 36 double, double Ds, if you allow it. But lucky you, you work hard in college and you are awarded an internship. No more waiting tables and selling peep dinner shows. It's the 80s and you are now working in a commercial photography studio in New York City. The photographer you work for has department store clients! This is the big time. You are finally working as a professional—a photography assistant. You call your parents, and they tell you they are proud of you, and warn you to be careful when you leave campus because there are a lot of crazy people in New York City. They jinx your internship. There are crazy people in New York City. One crazy was your boss, who without even asking, lifted your shirt and bra in one fell swoop and tried to devour your boob. You left the job and him without a chance for him to come back for seconds.

You are tired of the sleazy photographers in NYC, so in 1985 you change careers to an industry where you can express your frustrated feelings about not–so–fine fellows—acting. Eventually, almost a decade later, you move your off–off Broadway theatre skills to Hollywood. There, to pay the bills, you solicit tips in a red and white short–skirted–cheerleading waitress outfit. This was their required uniform at the 50s diner, along with frilly white ankle socks and saddle shoes. Your old manager follows you around as if he's a young football buck. Terrifying you in the walk–in refrigerator, he grabs you from behind, cups your breasts and bites the back of your neck. If you were ever going to brain anyone, this was the guy to smack over the head with the side of beef hanging next to you. Instead, you pick your battles. You act surprised—as if it's all fun and games in the cooler.

Then, one fine day it happens, you use your boobs for something different. It's 2002, a year after the Twin Towers fell. A time when time stopped and the world needed nursing too. The stress of having a baby at an advanced maternal age brings you to your knees. It's exhausting, it's frightening, it's all new to you. You need a lactation specialist, which makes you feel defective. You wonder why after all the shame and pain the jugs don't instinctually do what they are supposed to do! You look down at your newborn infant son and see your entire breast is covering his face. You think that maybe he can't breathe, so you push down the top half of your breast. Now you can see his nose and his eyes. He stares at you while finally sucking greedy gulps. Eureka! You smile down on him and realize this is a boob's job.

Also from Pure Slush Books

https://pureslush.com/store/

  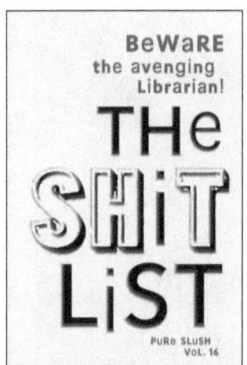

 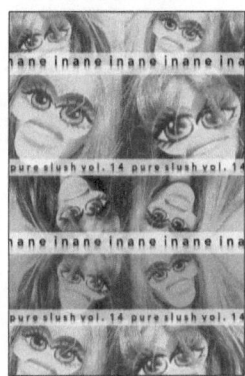 

- The Tyranny of Bacon Pure Slush Vol. 18
  ISBN: 978−1−922427−02−1 (paperback) / 978−1−922427−03−8 (eBook)
- The Beautifullest Pure Slush Vol. 17
  ISBN: 978−1−925536−23−2 (paperback) / 978−1−925536−24−9 (eBook)
- The Shitlist Pure Slush Vol. 16
  ISBN: 978−1−925536−90−4 (paperback) / 978−1−925536−91−1 (eBook)
- Happy^2 Pure Slush Vol. 15
  ISBN: 978−1−925536−39−3 (paperback) / 978−1−925536−40−9 (eBook)
- Inane Pure Slush Vol. 14
  ISBN: 978−1−925536−17−1 (paperback) / 978−1−925536−18−8 (eBook)
- Summer Pure Slush Vol. 12
  ISBN: 978−1−925536−13−3 (paperback) / 978−1−925536−14−0 (eBook)

Also from Pure Slush Books

https://pureslush.com/store/

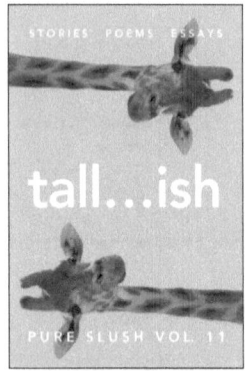

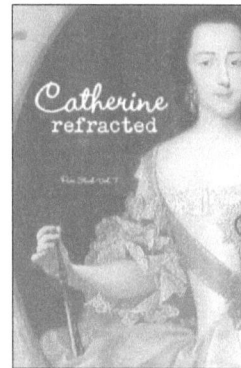
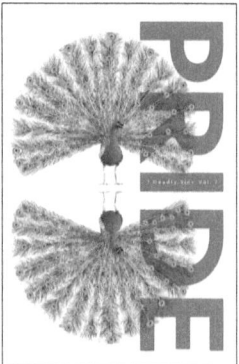

• tall…ish Pure Slush Vol. 11

ISBN: 978−1−925101−80−5 (paperback) / 978−1−925101−98−0 (eBook)

• Five Pure Slush Vol. 10

ISBN: 978−1−925101−71−3 (paperback) / 978−1−925101−72−0 (eBook)

• Feast Pure Slush Vol. 9

ISBN: 978−1−925101−63−8 (paperback) / 978−1−925101−66−9 (eBook)

• Barcode Pure Slush Vol. 8

ISBN: 978−1−925101−00−3 (paperback) / 978−1−925101−01−0 (eBook)

• Catherine refracted Pure Slush Vol. 7

ISBN: 978−1−925101−78−2 (paperback) / 978−1−925101−79−9 (eBook)

• Pride 7 Deadly Sins Vol. 7

ISBN: 978−1−925536−72−0 (paperback) / 978−1−925536−73−7 (eBook)

Also from Pure Slush Books

https://pureslush.com/store/

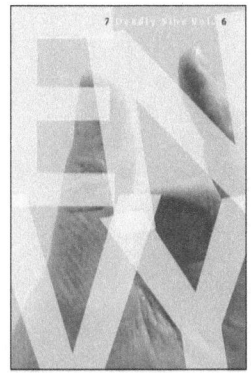

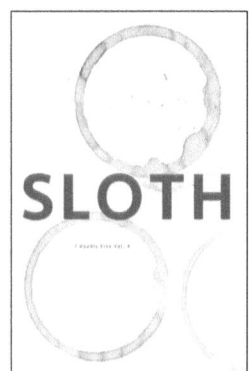

www.ingramcontent.com/pod-product-compliance
Lightning Source LLC
Chambersburg PA
CBHW020642260626
47157CB00008B/2868